# A WOMAN TRAPPED

# A WOMAN TRAPPED

## A WOMAN LOST SERIES BOOK 8

TB MARKINSON

Published by T. B. Markinson
Visit T. B. Markinson's official website at lesbianromancesbytbm.com for the latest news, book details, and other information.
Copyright © T. B. Markinson, 2020
Cover Design by: Erin Dameron-Hill
Edited by Kelly Hashway

This e-book is copyrighted and licensed for your personal enjoyment only. All rights reserved. No part of this publication may be reproduced, stored in a retrieval system, or transmitted in any forms or by any means without the prior permission of the copyright owner. The moral rights of the author have been asserted.

This book is a work of fiction. Names, characters, businesses, places, events, and incidents are the product of the author's imagination or are used fictitiously. Any resemblance to actual persons, living or dead, events, or locales is entirely coincidental.

LET'S KEEP IN TOUCH

One of the best parts of publishing is getting to know *you*, the reader.

My favorite method of keeping in touch is via my newsletter, where I share about my writing life, my cat (whom I lovingly call the Demon Cat since she hissed at me for the first forty-eight hours after I adopted her), upcoming new releases, promotions, and giveaways.

And, I give away two e-books to two newsletter subscribers every month. The winners will be able to choose from my backlist or an upcoming release.

I love giving back to you, which is why if you join my newsletter, I'll send you a free e-copy of *A Woman Lost*, book 1 of the A Woman Lost series, and bonus chapters you can't get anywhere else.

Also, you'll receive a free e-copy of *Tropical Heat*, a short story that lives up to the "heat" in its name.

If you want to keep in touch, sign up here: http://eepurl.com/hhBhXX

## A NOTE ABOUT A WOMAN TRAPPED

When I published *A Woman Complete*, book 7 in the A Woman Lost series, I didn't intend to write another Lizzie book. Even after I received countless emails from readers asking, some begging, for me to continue the series.

I was adamant, though, about turning the page on Lizzie.

Then COVID-19 started, and as it dragged on, I wondered which of my characters from my different series would freak out the most by the pandemic.

It didn't take me long to figure out Lizzie was my best bet. She struggles in normal situations, and 2020 was anything but normal.

My brain kept trying to figure out what Lizzie would say or do. Also, there was another aspect of Lizzie's character many readers asked me about, but I didn't know the answer. So, I started to dig into some research. Since I don't want to ruin the story, I won't say about what.

But I should note Lizzie is only starting to figure some things out, and as she learns more, perhaps she'll return to share with us.

As for now, I hope you enjoy Lizzie's bumpy return.

## CHAPTER ONE

I got out of my dad's car, his chauffeur pulling my bag from the trunk. It would have easily fit in the back seat next to me, but apparently, that was a foul when being driven. Something I wasn't used to at all. I could count on one hand how many rideshares I'd experienced, and after living in Fort Collins, Colorado for most of my adult life, I never really rode in cabs.

"Thank you, Matthew." I grabbed the handle to my carry-on luggage and slipped my laptop bag over my shoulder.

"Good luck getting home." He dipped his head in his subservient way that always made me uncomfortable.

"I may need it." I put my hand out, which he shook. "Please take care of yourself. I'm not sure what any of us would do if something happened to you."

He blinked away a tear. "Same to you."

I hadn't been kidding, because imagining my father, Charles Allen Petrie, behind the wheel was a terrifying prospect. He was a business mogul, but his survival skills when it came to ordinary life were subpar at best. I mean, *I* was more adept for the real world, and that wasn't saying much.

Clueless was the word commonly associated with me, and I was starting to wear it as a badge of honor because it really was my personality. It'd taken me over three decades to learn to like myself, but I think I was finally starting to get the hang of it.

It helped that I had an amazing wife who loved my quirks, and she made me see the good in those oddities, not the bad. Growing up, most of those in my life made me feel like such a loser, or worse yet, a complete failure for processing things differently and slowly. Sarah once said she loved seeing the lightbulb finally go off over my head because I got an excited look like a puppy going for a walk.

After several seconds, Matthew skirted around me and got into the car. I was never very effective at goodbyes, unsure when it was okay to end my habit of intense eye contact and turn my back. Luckily, he let me off the hook, or I would have stood there trying to come up with fifty different versions of *goodbye* and *stay safe*, each attempt getting progressively more excruciating and humiliating than the last.

I dashed into Denver International Airport, scanning the signs for the check-in area for my airline. Finding it, I entered my details into one of the computers, having to hit the backspace key a few times. My hands were normally unsteady on a good day due to my wacky thyroid levels, but today they were much shakier. Like my life depended on getting on the plane. It wasn't quite that drastic, but my marriage may reach a perilous stage if I missed the flight.

My phone rang as I hit the print button for my boarding pass.

"Are you on the plane yet?" Sarah asked in a tone that reinforced the feeling that my marriage did indeed hinge on getting back home. If she had it her way, I'd hop onto a magic carpet and be there in an enchanted jiffy. It was oddly funny, albeit confusing, when I was the rational one and Sarah was on the edge of sanity, and I had to really try to curb my laughter. Was that how she felt when the roles were reversed? If so, how did she prevent herself from laughing at me nearly every day?

"I'm printing my boarding pass." I pulled the paper from the machine.

"Can you hurry up, please?" Her voice contained a mixture of bossiness and desperation.

Confused, and annoyed, by her suggestive tone that I was being overly stubborn when she was being irrational (knowing she was being illogical didn't necessarily equate to me brushing it off because that wasn't my personality), I said, "My flight doesn't take off for a few hours. I sent you the details."

"I know, but this situation is making me nervous. I don't want you getting trapped in Denver."

"Domestic travel hasn't been banned. Only international flights from Europe and China." I made my way to security, managing my luggage with one hand while I pressed the phone to my right ear.

"Things are changing fast. I don't want to risk anything. You cannot leave me to take care of four kids, not to mention a cat and dog, all on my own."

Maddie, our friend, lived with us, so she wouldn't be completely alone. However, I was aware I shouldn't point that out. Not when Sarah was like this. "Let me call you back. This place is deserted, so I should sail through security."

There was a sudden absence of sound in my ear.

Sarah wasn't taking any risks about me missing the plane bound for Boston. The past week had been filled with madness. A handful of days ago, before I traveled to Colorado to see family and to attend a history conference over my university's spring break, Sarah was joking about the unfolding crisis, as if nothing serious would result, aside from some irrational tweets from a certain someone who was unhinged during the best of times.

The day I left, the president's chatter about the virus revolved around it being a hoax. I never ascribed to that notion since I'd been following the happenings in China from the beginning. Or at least since the news had started trickling out. Unfortunately, I hadn't factored in how quickly things would devolve in the US.

Within a day of my trip, the New York governor declared a state of emergency. Then the World Health Organization declared a pandemic. The following day, March Madness was cancelled. Soon after, Massachusetts declared a state of emergency, and public transportation was severely reduced.

In the middle of all of this, I'd gotten an email from my university that the college classes I taught were moving entirely online, something I'd never done before. The phrases *shelter in place* and *work from home* became more prominent in all sectors.

Everyone was scrambling to stock up on toilet paper, home office furniture, and sweatpants.

During all this insanity, the US banned foreigners from flying into the country, but it was rolled out in the worst way possible, causing Americans living and visiting abroad to panic buy tickets, resulting in them flooding airports. Mixing crowds and an airborne virus were the ingredients for an epic disaster.

Last night, when I was at dinner with my father and his wife, Sarah called, screaming for me to get back pronto. I tried pointing out that I was currently in Colorado, a part of the United States, and I was heading home in under two full days, but she wouldn't listen to reason. Under duress, I changed my flight to fifteen hours before my original one, and now I stood with my hands and feet out, for a TSA woman to use the wand to see why the metal detector had pinged.

"Can I pat down your legs?" she asked.

I nodded, but I had a feeling I really didn't have a say in the matter.

She started touching me, focusing more on the lower portion of my left calf, much to my relief. I wasn't the type who liked being manhandled by strangers. The good thing about the pandemic was not having to shake hands with strangers. I totally hated that, even if mine was strong so the other person wouldn't think me weak. And, I really struggled with the kissing of cheeks some visiting European professors did. Was I supposed to air kiss? Make contact? Once? Twice? I much preferred having an invisible three-foot barrier around me at all times, and when people invaded my space, it put me on high alert.

Finally, the TSA person waved me through. I gathered my gray trays from the conveyor belt and moved to the designated area to put my belt, hoodie, and shoes back on. After easing my laptop into the backpack along with the liquids in a plastic bag, I took a seat on a metal bench to finish getting things back on me or in their proper places.

Before I could finish, my phone was ringing again.

"Are you on the plane?"

"Sarah, honey, we only spoke a few minutes ago. I just cleared security and only have one shoe on." I tried to use my soothing voice, but my nerves were fraying as well, mostly because she was harassing me about something I had zero control over. I couldn't get my flight to leave early. What was she expecting from me?

"If you don't get on that plane, I want a divorce."

"Sounds drastic considering I'm not in charge of the shitstorm called COVID-19." I slid into my other shoe.

"Try me."

Again, there was a dial tone.

Before my trip, I'd been reading about the virus and had proposed cancelling my plans. Sarah laughed it off and said I was being dramatic. She really didn't want to hear comparisons to the great influenza of 1918. Granted, my knowledge of it was iffy at best. That didn't stop me from trying to spout facts. Would she listen? Nope. Instead, she wore the *don't give me a history lecture* look. So I did my best to curb my instinct. Now she'd been haranguing me nonstop for almost a full day because this was the earliest I could book a flight.

The irony was I hadn't wanted to leave in the first place, but she insisted I go to see my family and visit my brother in prison. Saying it was important for me to keep those connections alive since I could be the out of sight, out of mind type. I would have loved to point out all of that, but during the course of our marriage, I've learned it was best not to crow too much when she'd been in the wrong. It killed me, not getting credit nor being able to say one of my all-time favorite lines: *I told you so!* But was it worth not seeing her naked for the foreseeable future?

No, most definitely not.

My nickname for her was *Sexy Sarah* for two reasons. She was totally hot, and I wasn't very creative when it came to nicknames. I kinda called them like I saw them.

I jammed my arms into my green Colorado State hoodie, zipping it up halfway, and then rang her back. When she snapped *what*, I simply said, "I love you, and I'll be home tonight."

She started to cry.

Yep, I'd definitely made the right call not rubbing her nose in it.

"Sweetheart, listen to me," I said, consulting my watch. "Everything is going to be fine. My flight boards in one hour and thirty-eight minutes. The flight time is three hours and forty-seven minutes." I added the sums, tapping my thumb and index fingers together as I did so. "That means approximately in five and a half hours, I think, I'll touch down in Boston. The drive home is roughly thirty minutes."

"That's over six hours from now. Who knows what will change while you're in the air?"

I'd had a similar thought but didn't want to pile on to her stress. "Nothing will happen. A week ago, the president was saying this was all fake news."

"He's the problem. His impulses wreck everything." I could picture her pacing our Wellesley kitchen in her slippers and robe.

"Honey, let's focus on you, the kids, and getting me home. Those are the things we can control."

"I should have listened to you."

"I'm sorry. Can you repeat that?" I couldn't help the smile from forming on my lips or keep from punching the air with a victorious fist. Thank goodness we weren't on a video call, because those actions would have gotten me into serious hot water.

"No!"

"That's a good sign!" I did another fist bump, feeling at ease with her snark. I could handle that from a distance. Panicking Sarah was much harder to manage.

I couldn't stop smiling, and an employee at a restaurant gave me an odd look. Her face conveyed nothing good would ever happen again.

I continued, "It's after ten at night there. Go to bed, and I'll wake you when I get home."

"Can you talk to me for a bit longer?"

I squeezed my luggage between my barstool and the empty one next to me and set my backpack on the chair. I covered the mouthpiece of the phone and said, "Hot tea, please," to the bartender. My evening pills alarm went off, so I added a glass of water to my order. Then I said to Sarah, "Sure. Whatever you need, I'll do it."

"I need you to be here."

"Working on it, honey." I pulled my pill organizer from my backpack.

"You keep calling me honey."

"You're acting irrational." That had slipped out, and I squeezed my eyes shut, waiting for the inevitable Sarah squawk. I popped my calcium and multivitamin into my mouth and chased them down with a long tug of water.

Fortunately for me, she laughed and squeaked out, "I know."

"I understand. If I was facing being on my own for who knows how long with our brood, I'd be acting the same way."

"Why is the world going to shit?" There was such a profound sense of defeat in her words.

"Don't ask a historian that unless you want a lecture dating back to the beginning of time."

"Will it put me to sleep?"

"Oh, hey. There's an idea." I snapped my fingers and looked around the terminal. "It's dead here. I've never been in an airport without passengers. The word *eerie* doesn't even begin to describe it." I stopped myself from saying it seemed like the end of the world.

"Maybe your flight will be empty."

"I hope so. I'm not in the mood to be around *people*." I squirmed on the barstool.

"Let's go back to the lecture." She yawned. "Put me to sleep."

\*\*\*

After cramming a bag into the overhead compartment, I placed my backpack in the middle seat, sidestepped my way to the window, and sank into the chair, relief flooding me that I was finally on the effing plane.

There was a trickle of passengers coming down the aisle, but I kept an eagle eye for potential row mates. It was something I always did whenever I flew anywhere, but this seemed like the best chance to have an entire row to myself. Even the seats on the other side of the walkway were person-free. The introvert inside me was doing the merriest of happy dances. Although, why couldn't I get on an earlier flight? Was the airline limiting seats, or was this one not a popular time?

Right when I thought I was in the clear, a man with a prominent unibrow stood staring at his ticket and then up at the number above the seats. Still, he asked, "Is this row seventeen?"

I nodded, swallowing the words, "Take a hike, mister."

"I have the middle seat." He pointed at my bag.

I peered around him and saw the seats across the way were still empty and the cabin crew was in the process of shutting the doors. "Besides you, I think everyone is seated. No one's over there." I pointed across from me. "Just to be safe, considering the pandemic, ya know." I wasn't entirely sure the man knew anything about COVID since he was standing so close to me, breathing through his mouth.

"That's my seat, though." He indicated the middle seat again, unable to take his eyes off of my bag in his chair.

*Seriously, dude. Even I'm not this clueless.*

I started to reach for my face in exasperation but stopped myself in time. Not touching your face was one of the new rules.

"Okay. Whatever." I stood and grabbed my bag, asking gruffly, "Would you mind letting me out?"

He stepped back a row, and I moved to the other side of the plane, taking the window seat. He gaped at me as if I was breaking a consecrated flying rule before he eased into his assigned middle seat and clicked his seatbelt into place, sitting rigidly, staring straight ahead. He didn't have any baggage with him. Did he check a bag? How many people didn't bring a thing on the plane?

One of the flight attendants who'd witnessed the interaction winked at me as she walked by. There was no way in hell, I could do her job. People ruined everything.

Before the plane taxied, I dashed off a text to Sarah, wishing her sweet dreams. She didn't respond before I switched off the phone.

We took off, and after twenty minutes, I crammed the book I was attempting to read for work back into my bag and cued up *Crazy Rich Asians*. Every time I laughed out loud into my elbow, the man in the middle seat turned to me with a dazed expression. I was starting to worry about him.

Did he need a minder? Would Sarah kill me if I brought him home like a stray puppy? Not that I would, but the image made me smile.

I ended up drifting off into an uncomfortable sleep, forgetting about everything until we landed. After escaping the plane, I never saw the man again, which gave me pause.

Had he even existed?

More importantly, would the world return to normal, or was everything about to disturb my tenuous grip on reality? I wasn't the type to easily adapt to changes. What was in store for me? Did I really want to know?

CHAPTER TWO

Arriving home, I tiptoed into the bedroom and quietly changed into pajamas. After brushing and flossing, I climbed into bed, trying my best not to disturb Sarah. I had said I'd wake her when I got home, but she was completely passed out, and judging by the crinkles in her forehead, it hadn't been an easy task to get some much-needed shut-eye.

Waking her seemed like the wrong choice. Of course, I'd probably pay for that decision later, but I was used to Sarah getting mad, and I felt completely justified in this situation, although I'd do my best not to tell her that.

The problem with always thinking I was right was not everyone agreeing with me. It irritated me to no end that they were so determined to be outright wrong. Although, I'd sorta become accustomed to it, so I stopped pointing it out at every possible opportunity. It was better to pick and choose certain battles. On most occasions, I succeeded but not always because I gotta be me, meaning I loved to cloak myself with righteousness.

I still put one arm around Sarah, though, and eased the creases in her forehead with gentle strokes of my free hand. She snuggled closer against me. As I lay there in our bed in our relatively new home (to us, not brand-spanking new construction), I couldn't focus on sleep but on all of the craziness happening around us.

When I was a history undergraduate, some of my classes touched on the great influenza of 1918, but I couldn't recall all the details. At one point, years ago, I'd purchased a paperback on the subject by John M. Barry, but I didn't remember seeing it after the move nor could I recall entering it into my spreadsheet I'd started after the move because I was absolutely convinced at least one box of books had been lost. This was yet another mental tick in the *I was right, dammit!* column.

I one-clicked the audiobook on my phone, unfortunately though, my Bose headphones weren't in their usual place in the drawer of my nightstand since I hadn't unpacked before getting into bed, and I didn't want to wake Sarah by removing my arm. Which meant I had to resist starting my research right then and there. Besides, it was late, and I felt like I'd been up for twenty-four hours straight, even if I'd caught some Zs on the flight. Sleep on a plane hardly ever felt restful, and I couldn't kick the feeling that the new normal would be anything but for a long time to come.

* * *

"Lizzie!"

I tried rousing from a dream where a man with a unibrow kept randomly appearing needing help, but I was never able to do anything for him.

"Wake up!"

Someone was jostling my arm. "What's wrong?"

"You didn't wake me." Sarah, sitting up in bed with her arms crossed, glared down at me.

"So, you got even by waking me." I rolled onto my back, yawning. "Full disclosure: I knew you'd be mad when I made the executive decision." Damn. I had told myself not to point that out. Perhaps I was terrible at picking my battles.

"Why did you make that decision on your own?" She slanted her head, causing dark hair to cascade, framing her face just so, reminding me how lucky I was to have such a stunning woman yelling at me in our bed.

"You looked exhausted," I explained and yawned again, much wider this time.

"You look like you've been through ten rounds with Mike Tyson." Her dark chocolate eyes softened.

"Kinda feel like it. Are you okay?" I reached for her with my hand.

Sarah stared at me. "I don't know how to answer that. Are you okay?"

"I'm home. As for okay, who the hell knows?" I didn't speak to all the thoughts swirling through my mind, but not saying them didn't appease the worry in either of us.

Her brow furrowed again with apprehension as she nodded.

My eyelids sagged shut, and I started to drift off again.

"We need to stock up on food," Sarah said, rousing me back from sleep.

"Make me a list, and I'll go to the store later today," I said, trying to fight off another wave of exhaustion.

A weird expression crossed her face. "Are you insane? There's a global pandemic. The world is shutting down!"

"We still need to eat." I didn't think I had to point that out, but to be safe, I did. She still seemed highly unreasonable, and I was hoping she'd snap out of it soon. I was book smart, hence the middle of the night purchase of *The Great Influenza* book. Sarah was the one who kept the Petrie household running like a well-oiled machine. I could not be trusted with that responsibility.

"I'm not sending you to the store."

"Well, I'm not going to reenact the Donner Party."

"Yes, that's the idea I had in mind. Culling the

Petrie herd one leg bone at a time." She mimed eating one corncob style, which confused me.

I blinked and let out a whoosh of air. "Did you wake me simply to yell at me?"

"Seems like it." She gave a *what can you do* shrug.

I opened my arms. "Come here. Let's cuddle and figure out groceries later."

"I wish you'd woken me when you got home."

"Would it have stopped the yelling? I'm not in the mood for it." I wiped some sleep from my eyes.

"I'm sorry. I don't know how to handle this."

"No one does." I swiveled my head to my old-fashioned ticking alarm clock on my nightstand, remembering my book on the history of time that was possibly on the MIA list. "It's barely five. Let's get some rest before we boldly start our new lives in this chaos."

CHAPTER THREE

Around ten in the morning, I sat on one of the barstools at the kitchen island, nursing my third cup of tea. Sarah had let me sleep in after I fell back into a deep, but fitful slumber. "What exactly do we need from the store? After some googling, I've learned I can order from an app called Instacart."

"Everything," Sarah said, holding Calvin close to her chest, bobbing up and down. I wasn't sure if the action was to settle our youngest child or her own rattled nerves.

"O-ookay." Obviously, she wasn't going to offer her usual explicit directions, like organic salted farm fresh butter that was churned by virgins during a blue moon. "I'll go through the last four months of lists you've given me and compile the order."

"You keep every grocery list?"

"Yes. In my phone." I held it in the air as proof

even though she wasn't asking for any. It was the historian in me, and I tended to footnote my footnotes. Many accused me of being a know-it-all, but it was simply something I couldn't curb. I loved being right and having others know it, which probably meant my accusers were justified. Uh… I needed to mull this over more—

"Why do I provide you with a new list, then?" A bewildered crease settled between Sarah's eyebrows.

"Uh… you're bossy?" I spoke with exactly the right amount of fear in my voice, which I'd mastered over the years to be able to speak the truth without eliciting too much screeching from her.

This morning, though, she simply shrugged a shoulder.

I did a mental fist pump, but also worried about her frayed nerves over the long term. If push came to shove, I could run this family for a day or two at most. While I was able to do a lot of my lecture prep in my home office to help out with simple things like diaper changes, I wasn't the parent who knew the ins and outs of how the household ran. Even when I was single and living in an apartment, I had a housecleaner. My ultimate goal in life was to have a nanny for *me*, not the children, because I needed someone to tell me what to do and when. And to pick out my outfits for when I had to make an impression. A good one, not what I usually accomplished on my own.

Oh shit, our new housecleaner probably wouldn't

be able to report to duty twice a week. I added cleaning supplies to the list.

Freddie, one of our toddlers, tugged on the hem of my shirt. "Read, please."

I took his book and then lifted him into my lap. "First, help me place the food order."

"F-fud." He giggled and squirmed on my lap because I tickled his side.

"Yes, food." I kissed the top of his head, his blond hair turning more brownish like my mousy shade. "You're the easygoing one in the family. You and Demi."

He leaned against me, raising his arms up around my neck. "Hug!"

I squeezed him tightly for several moments.

Sarah smiled, looking not as stressed. Our kids, when being cute and cuddly, had that effect on both of us.

"Alright, little man. Let's get this done to help Mommy. She's losing her mind," I dramatically whispered to Fred, with every intention of being overheard since I knew he wouldn't really know what I was talking about.

"I can hear you." Sarah's sing-song voice was a warning, and she made a show of still bobbing up and down with Calvin. "Remember the *no fighting* rule in front of the kids."

"Remember the *always tell the truth* rule." I used my own singsong voice and offered her a wide grin.

Tucking my head down, I started to input the order into the freshly downloaded app on my iPad, which was synced with my phone.

After five minutes, Fred wanted off my lap, taking his book with him.

Another hour passed before I announced, "By Jove, I think I got everything! We have stuff coming from different stores, and I'm glad I stocked up on TP in Denver. That box should be arriving in a week or so."

"You shipped toilet paper from Denver?" Sarah gave me an incredulous look.

I nodded. "Three whole boxes. Along with wet wipes and diapers." I blew on my knuckles and shined them on the front of my sweater.

"Look at you!" Sarah, child-free at the moment, kissed my cheek. "Oh, did you get organic sweet potato veggie chips? They're my new addiction."

I blinked.

"I take that as a no." Her smile fell.

"It wasn't on any of my previous lists, but…" I checked the text messages on my phone. "None of our shoppers has started yet, so I can still add it." I threaded my fingers and stretched them like an athlete before the start of a race. "Watch the food shopping pro handle this."

After a few clicks, I bragged, "Your request has been added, your Royal Highness. Anything else?"

"Did you get me a surprise?" She batted her lashes at me.

"What surprise?"

"You are aware of the definition, aren't you?" Sarah playfully jutted out a hip.

I snapped my fingers. "I got it!"

A couple more clicks, and I amended the order for a different store. "Oh boy, are you going to be surprised!"

Sarah rolled her eyes, but her lighthearted laughter was a relief.

I got off the barstool. "Now, if you'll excuse me, I have a reading date with our children because I'm the number one parent in this household."

"Yeah, yeah." She turned to leave the kitchen. "I'm going to take a shower."

Calvin started to cry.

Sarah whirled around. "That's his hungry cry. Oh, Number One Parent, can you feed our youngest?"

I opened the fridge door, bending over for a better look. "Is there a snack prepared?"

"Nope."

"But... Fred wants me to read to him, and he's already waited for over an hour."

"Are you playing favorites?" This time when she jutted out her hip, she meant it.

"You know I don't, and I hate it when you accuse me of it." I stuck my tongue out at her.

"What can I say? I like getting you hot and bothered." Sarah hunched down and asked Fred, who'd wandered into the kitchen when he heard his name, "You want Mommy to read you a book?"

He nodded so sincerely no one could say no, aside from sociopaths, and Sarah didn't fit the bill.

"Looks like you've been relieved from snack duty." She started to prepare food for all of the kids, since when one received something, it set off a domino effect.

I took Freddie's hand, and we settled on the floor in a cozy beanbag in the corner of the front room. "Okay, Fred. Which book?"

He pointed to the stack next to us, and I took the top one. *"The Very Hungry Caterpillar.* Seems fitting, considering."

I finished that book, and the kids ate their snack, while I read another story. After that one, Olivia and Demi retreated to the art table with Maddie, their unofficial aunt who lived with us. We adopted Demi after her mother died and my brother, Demi's father, was sent to prison.

Freddie asked for one more story, and we continued to snuggle in the beanbag. He loved to turn the page when I gave a slight nod of the head.

My phone vibrated. "Great news. Our shopper has started on the BJ's list."

Sarah, freshly showered, smiled appreciatively, cuddling a now sleeping Calvin in the leather chair.

A few more minutes passed, and I got another alert. "Shaw's is in progress!"

"Look at you. Grocery shopping and reading to our son. You're taking multitasking to the next level." Sarah sounded exhausted, and she leaned her head back on the chair.

"I wonder what else I can tackle at the same time."

"There's a ton of laundry that needs doing," Maddie said.

"Oh, we're low on detergent. Did you get some?" Sarah asked.

"Yep!"

"Maybe this will become one of your permanent jobs." Sarah resettled her head against the chair, and I wondered how much sleep she'd lost while I was in Colorado. Should I point out if she spent less time screaming at me on the phone, she could have rested? Probably not.

My phone buzzed again, and I read the text. Then I read it again. "That's weird. I guess our first BJ's shopper dropped out because now it says Richard is doing it."

Sarah bunched her brow, but didn't open her eyes. "I wonder why."

I shrugged.

Freddie wobbled over to join the art crew, Maddie giving him a high five, one of the greetings he loved.

My phone went off again. "Oh, same thing with Shaw's."

"What?" Sarah asked, now in the process of trying to sip her coffee without disturbing Calvin.

"We got a new shopper. Well…" I raked a hand through my short hair, rustling up the cowlick on the back of my head. "At least they stay on top of it."

Sarah now wore a dubious expression, the one that said, *I don't know how you screwed up, but you did.*

I tried blocking it out of my mind, but after a second, I couldn't resist digging deeper to see what was going on. I went back to my iPad still on the kitchen counter, typed in my password, and clicked on the orders tab. A few more clicks and I uttered, "Uh-oh."

Sarah craned her head to see me in the kitchen. "What's wrong, Number One Mom?"

"It's quite possible when I amended the orders I created duplicates instead." I carried the iPad into the room and took my seat by the fireplace.

"Are you saying four shoppers are now wandering the aisles for you in BJ's and Shaw's?"

I nodded.

I received another text. "Oh, Richard can't find the bagels and wants to know if English muffins will do."

"I guess so. How many bags of bagels did you request?"

"Five."

Sarah's mouth formed an O.

"Now, Sean can't find cottage cheese and wants to know if yogurt will do?"

"How much cottage cheese did you order?"

"I rather not say." I avoided her eyes.

Maddie let out a whistle but kept her focus on the kids, helping Freddie use a glue stick.

"Let me see if I'm understanding this. You've placed an insane grocery order to get us through a few months, and you have two shoppers in each store competing against the other, causing them to scrounge for replacements we don't actually need." Sarah sounded baffled and amused.

"Um… it's quite possible that's what's going on." I okayed a few more substitutions, the messages lighting up my phone like a slot machine in Vegas.

"Why don't you cancel two of the orders?"

"Because they already started and they're trying hard to fulfill the orders. Sean says the manager is looking in the back for more cottage cheese."

"He's a go-getter." I still couldn't determine if Sarah was more impressed or annoyed by the situation.

"It might be because I gave each a hundred-dollar tip to jump the line." I didn't look up, but Sarah groaned, so I defended, "The app suggested providing a large tip to garner attention. Competition is fierce these days, and you wouldn't let me do the shopping on my own. I've read reports some are waiting weeks for delivery."

"I'm questioning letting you do anything on your own ever again." Sarah rubbed her eyes.

"Do the kids like Club crackers over Saltines?" My

fingers hovered over my phone, waiting for my instruction.

"Oh, no. This is all you. Make the decisions."

"I prefer Club if anyone cares," Maddie piped up.

I gnashed my teeth at her but okayed Club as the substitute and then asked Sarah, "What happened to you not trusting me to do anything on my own? You literally just said it."

"It's too much fun watching you squirm right now." She took another sip from her coffee, seeming more alive than minutes earlier.

Maddie nodded. "This is the most fun I've had since the pandemic started, which seems like years ago."

"Et tu, Brute." I feigned being shocked but wasn't since Maddie was a pot stirrer.

Maddie laughed.

Forty-five minutes passed, and I got the alert that the first BJ's shopper was en route. Less than five minutes later, the other shopper from the same store was also on their way.

I filled Sarah in on all the developments. "Do you think they'll bump into each other at the front door?"

"I really hope so." She tapped her fingertips together.

"Wait? Are you cheering against me now?" My phone buzzed. "The first Shaw's person is on their way. Sh-shiitake! Will all of them meet up?"

"Too bad there's a pandemic. We could invite them in for a party."

Maddie burst into laughter but didn't add any commentary. Did that mean she actually felt sorry for me, or was the art project that riveting?

"Oh, so funny," I said to Sarah and then groaned when my phone buzzed again.

"Are all four on their way?" Sarah was enjoying herself way too much.

"It'll be five, actually. I had to make a Hannaford's order for some of the organic stuff you like. Luckily, I didn't amend that order, so there's only one shopper—" My phone buzzed yet again. "Who is on her way."

She laughed when I released an anguished sigh and swiped my forehead with the back of my hand.

"At least we won't starve," I said, trying to see the bright side.

"I'm curious where everything will go. We only have one extra fridge in the basement."

"I told you we should have gotten a large freezer."

"I didn't know the world was going to end."

"I've been warning you about this since February!" I flung a hand in the air. "You never listen to me."

"You've been talking about the end of days for as long as I've known you. You're a historian of the Nazis. Nothing you study is cheerful."

"I also told you we should build a bunker."

"If I remember correctly, you wanted a moat filled with alligators and crocs around our house. Don't go changing your story to suit the current situation." Her devilish grin turned me on, and from the glimmer in her eyes, she knew it.

There was a knock on the door, and I started to count. One Mississippi. Two Mississippi. The instructions on the app had been clear: the transfer should be no-contact.

Ten Mississippi...

"Will you help me to avoid having the drivers bump into each other?" I asked Sarah, getting to my feet.

I got to fifteen Mississippi.

Sarah handed Calvin to Maddie.

"Twenty Mississippi!" I rushed to open the door and discovered boxes and boxes of food on the ground.

As soon as Sarah and I got them inside and the door clicked shut, I heard another person dropping off more food. Sarah went to open the door, but I stopped her and whispered, "It's contactless delivery."

After a hesitant knock, I placed my ear on the door and detected retreating footsteps. When I opened the door, there were more boxes than the last delivery, or so it seemed.

"You work on getting this away from the door, so I can bring this load in," I directed Sarah.

A car pulled up out front.

"Hurry!" I said, pulling three boxes in at once.

The person sat in the car, hunching over the

steering wheel, staring at me with a puzzled expression.

Getting everything inside, I closed the door and started clearing more room for the next round.

"We're getting a lot of food," I said when Sarah returned to the entryway, as if she didn't have eyeballs in her head.

"I see that. How much more are we expecting?"

"I really don't want to say. Can you start taking this somewhere so I can bring more boxes in?"

"Where do you want me to put it?" She sounded flummoxed.

"I don't know. The attic." I flicked a hand in the air, not wanting to be distracted by the details. Not while at DEFCON 5.

"Maybe we should build an igloo for the frozen stuff."

"Sadly, there isn't any snow on the ground or in the ten-day forecast."

"I was joking." She laughed. "I'm so glad you're supermom, and you have to put all of this away."

I scratched the back of my head, eyeing the contents on the floor. "I may need to order more storage containers."

"Oh no. I think you're ordering days are over. You tell me what you need, and I'll handle it. I don't even trust you one-clicking audiobooks." She kissed my cheek.

"I did that without any issues last night while you

were sleeping." I wasn't able to mount much defiance in my tone considering the mishap I was in the midst of.

There was another knock, and I got back to the task at hand.

CHAPTER FOUR

Someone tapped my shoulder, and I slid the headphones off my ears and onto my neck.

"Can you spare an orange?" Sarah smiled at me, fluttering her long lashes in a not so innocent way.

"Very funny, wise guy." I opened the fridge and pulled out one. "We have fifty pounds worth, so do you want two? Why not three? You can never have too much vitamin C, especially during these trying times."

"At least we won't get scurvy."

"There you go, finally finding the bright side to this!" I waved to all the items on every available surface in the kitchen. "You can fit a lot of fake meatballs into these little suckers." I held up one of the packed plastic containers, the red lid bulging upward slightly, but still secured.

"Do I even want to look in the freezer?" Her hand was on the door handle.

"If you do, I suggest opening it slowly and ensure no children or pets are underfoot." I scanned the area but didn't spy any of the kids, Hank, our black cat, or Gandhi, the demon Yorkie we adopted when George, our former neighbor in Colorado, was moved into a nursing home.

Sarah let her hand fall to her side. "Why don't we make you the freezer girl until we run out of food or this pandemic is over? Whichever happens first. I can get you an outfit."

"I was under the impression I couldn't be trusted with anything, but here I am putting everything away, and now I'm the freezer girl, which isn't a thing, you know."

"It's a thing now. I hate smashed toes. Besides, this is all your doing."

I shook a finger. "Oh no. You played a part. I had everything settled, but then you needed organic sweet potato veggie chips. After I took care of that, you requested a surprise. If not for those two additions, we wouldn't have two hundred and eighty-seven bagels, only one hundred and forty-four."

Sarah closed her eyes. "Twelve times twenty-four is two hundred and eighty-eight. You're off by one."

"I ate one. Putting all this away is making me hungry." I rubbed my stomach.

"Poor you." Her pat on my cheek lacked warmth.

I held the orange in my palm. "Do you want me to peel this for you or not?"

"I want to know what my surprise is." She pressed her palms together and stood on her tippy toes.

"I suggest being nice to me, or you'll never find out." I tossed the orange from one hand to the other.

Sarah wrapped her arms around my neck. "I'm always nice to you."

"Oh, please! You've been giving me shit since I got home from Denver. No, you started screaming at me on the phone, demanding I catch an earlier flight."

"Giving you a hard time is how I demonstrate my love and how much I missed you." She gazed at me under hooded eyes.

"Not sure I want to go on anymore business trips in the near future if you have to fill all the days I was gone with biting wit." I tried to make that come across as believable, because truth be known, her staring at me like that was revving my southern region engines to *man the torpedoes* level.

She gave me a quick peck on the lips. "Better?"

"I'm warming up to this approach." I tried kissing her again, but she ducked my smooch.

"I'm so thoughtful I'm going to ask you very nicely about Mom and Troy moving in for the duration of the pandemic." She tickled the hairs on the back of my neck, but my blood went cold. "Please say yes because I already told them they could, and they'll be arriving shortly with their stuff."

"W-What?" I stuttered. "Do you know the meaning of ask? This is more like informing me of how things will be. Laying down the Sarah Law." I made a line in the air with one hand.

"It's the only logical choice given the situation."

"What's the other option?"

"Since we don't know how long this will last, we might be prevented from going to each other's houses. It only makes sense for all of us to live under the same roof. Aren't you glad you got so much food?"

I swallowed and took a deep, steadying breath. Then another.

"Maddie has decided to stay here with us, not with her new girl." Sarah spoke as if this should appease my mind. "Five adults will get through this food pretty quickly."

"Let me see if I'm understanding everything that's being said. We'll be quarantining with Rose, Troy, Maddie, and our brood?"

Sarah nodded enthusiastically as if this should be the best news I've ever heard. After studying me for seven seconds, she added, "At least Allen headed back to Colorado to be with your dad and Helen."

As it turned out, my half brother had been flying in the opposite direction on the same night I returned since his university had gone remote like mine.

Given the situation, Sarah seemed way too gleeful. She got along with her mom, and when Sarah was eighteen and moved to Colorado to go to college, Rose moved there as well. They were super close, and the only wrinkle came about when Rose started dating

Troy, who was much younger than Rose. It was a bumpy introduction to the family, but Sarah finally accepted the kindhearted man. However, not once during our time together had Sarah ever hinted that she'd want her mom under the same roof aside from occasional meals. I would have remembered that. I think. I scanned my memory for any mention of this possibility but came up short. I mean, I hadn't considered a full-blown pandemic, so I didn't think I was at fault for not figuring out this situation.

"What are you on? You're way too happy." I lowered my face to see directly into her eyes.

"I'm not telling you," she teased.

"Fine. I'm going to turn my back for a second to get a plate from the cupboard. If you can place whatever happy pill you've obviously been hoarding into my tea, I'd be much obliged."

"Don't be that way. The kids will love having everyone here."

I groaned. "You always do that when I don't like something. Bring the kids into it so I can't say no."

"It's the reason I had them. Leverage over you. You're not easy to live with."

"Me?" I squealed, putting my hand over my heart. "You keep planning these family things that always backfire, or do I need to remind you of the Christmas party that ended with Peter going to prison?"

"I can't be blamed for Peter getting arrested. He brought that on himself."

"Still. It was a disaster."

She had the decency to nod in agreement.

The front door opened, and there was a much too cheerful, "Yoo-hoo!"

"Mom's here!" Sarah left me in the kitchen.

"I never said yes," I hollered after her, but it was a useless effort. Once Sarah set her mind on something, it would be easier to move a mountain than her opinion.

"Holy—" Maddie stopped saying the rest as she burst into the kitchen. "Sarah warned me it'd be a lot to witness now that all of it is in here, but I had no idea it was this bad."

"Think fast." I tossed the orange I never prepared for Sarah at Maddie, stopping myself from saying a third of the shopping orders had already been put away, making it even worse than she thought.

She caught it with one hand and started to speak, "At least—"

"We won't get scurvy. Sarah already used that one. Be cleverer." I butchered the last word as the noises from all the people in the house dramatically increased.

"I take it from your face you're only just hearing about the living arrangement." Maddie's expression softened as she placed the orange on top of a pile of five-pound bags of apples. I still needed to find a home for them, but they were hardier and didn't require refrigeration.

"I really have no idea what I did in my previous life, but I feel like I'm constantly being punished by those who claim to love me."

"Luckily for you, I've never claimed that." Maddie batted her eyelashes innocently. The women in my life were way too obvious when they wanted something from me.

"No!" I held a *stop right there* hand in the air.

"No what?" She continued feigning innocence.

"Whatever you're about to ask me, the answer is no." I jerked my head side to side so fast I made myself dizzy, but it was imperative to reinforce no matter what, I wasn't going to give in.

"Fine. I'll ask Sarah. She'll talk sense into you."

I pulled the back of her shirt, nearly strangling Maddie, but I didn't let go. "I said no."

"You don't wear the pants in this family." Maddie pretended to go left but then twirled away, breaking free from my grasp.

The orange rolled off the apples and plummeted to the floor.

CHAPTER FIVE

During dinner that night, the doorbell rang.

"Who can that be?" I looked up from my spaghetti and fake meatballs. "There's a pandemic. People shouldn't be ringing bells." My brain couldn't wrap around who in the hell was standing at my front door. Thanks to Sarah, all of our family in Massachusetts sat at the dinner table with me.

"I'll get it." Maddie excitedly hopped to her feet.

"Did someone order more food or something?" I asked Sarah, still not processing, even though from the look she gave me I was missing the obvious.

She shook her head, her eyes falling to her lap.

It wasn't like our doorbell rang much during normal times, but these were very strange times, and having someone at the door screamed, "You're not going to like this, Lizzie!"

Troy shifted in his seat and cleared his throat.

Rose bobbed Demi on her knee, going to great lengths to duck behind the child so I couldn't make eye contact.

Whatever was going on, everyone else knew but me. Meaning they all expected me to overreact in Lizzie fashion. I set down my fork, feeling as if I shouldn't have a weapon in my hand for what was about to be sprung on me.

Maddie walked into the dining room, holding hands with a woman who had dark, curly hair and startling blue eyes. Upon further scrutiny, they were more gray than blue, but large and penetrating.

"Everyone, this is Willow." Maddie raised their conjoined hands and gave the back of Willow's hand a kiss. "Our final roommate during this pandemic experience."

\* \* \*

SARAH SLINKED INTO THE BEDROOM, TRYING her best to look sexy but also repentant.

"Don't be mad," she said, putting up her hands.

"I'm not. I'm reading." I pointed to my headphones, hitting the pause button on my phone and shoving the left one off my ear, only willing to concede that much.

"What are you listening to?" She was doing her best to show interest.

"*Fascism* by Albright." She didn't need to read the book because she was a dictator through and through.

Sarah set something shiny on top of the dresser. "Haven't you read that one?" She proceeded to shed her jeans and undies and slipped on flannel pajama bottoms.

"Yes, but I'm relistening to a chapter to help me prepare a lecture." I moved the ear piece back into place and hit play, irked by everything that'd happened over the course of the day, especially the one thing that had sent me over the edge, but we hadn't had time to discuss it since the house was full of people!

I was still flabbergasted. In hindsight, I should have seen the big whammy coming from a mile away, given Sarah and Maddie were involved, but I'd blissfully blocked out the possibility. In a short conversation about the incident, Sarah said I'd met Willow, but I'm sure I would have remembered those eyes. Since moving to Wellesley, Maddie had dated a handful of women, so odds were Sarah was thinking of someone else.

Sarah sat down on the side of the bed next to me, motioning with one hand for me to take the headphones off completely.

I did, groaning. "I'm really not in the mood for a Sarah lecture."

"Wasn't planning one. Talk to me. I know you're upset that everyone is under our roof."

I massaged my eyes. "I'm not mad. Okay, that's a

lie. I am. Livid would be a better word. Also, I wish you didn't make these decisions without me."

"You weren't here." She tried sounding meek.

"It was still a big effing decision to make on your own." I drilled my eyes into hers.

"I know. I'm sorry. It's just—I panicked." She flicked a hand in the air.

"I'll buy that when it comes to your mom and Troy. But the other? That wasn't panic. You gave your blessing today, apparently while I was out on a walk with Gandhi and Fred."

"That was a pity yes. Maddie doesn't want to leave Demi, and she really likes this chick. She's a professor. You two can nerd out together." Sarah bumped my arm in a way that implied *wouldn't that be grand*, but I pulled away.

"Her name is Willow Greene. How can anyone take a woman seriously with a name like that? They basically mean the same thing."

"How do they mean the same thing?" Sarah's eyebrows twisted in confusion.

"Willows are in nature, and what do you see when in the great outdoors?" I waited for the lightbulb moment to go off over her head, but it didn't come. "Green."

"That's a stretch. Even for you."

"What do you mean *even for you?*"

"Lizzie, sweetheart—"

"I hate when you speak to me in that super calm,

*everything will be okay* voice when you think I'm being highly irrational."

"I'm doing no such thing." She continued to speak in the tone I hated. "Your initial reaction to any change is to slam on the brakes. Given this situation, we don't really have time to delay. Things are happening fast. Decisions have to be made on the spot."

"It's been well over forty-eight hours since you called me in a panic, and the entire country has not shut down. Not even our state."

"I brought you something to cheer you up." She opened her right hand, displaying a Hershey's Kiss.

"Where'd you find that?"

"In the pantry behind the flour."

"I hid the bag there!"

"Why?"

"It was your surprise. That bag of Kisses ended up costing us about five-hundred dollars when I accidentally duplicated the order."

Sarah started to say something, changed her mind, and then settled on the previous conversation. "Willow teaches history. It'll be good for you to have someone to talk to."

I took the Kiss and started to peel back the foil. "Please. She studies the Gilded Age. Granted, it's not as boring as Western history, which I couldn't stand especially when we lived in Fort Collins and everyone assumed I studied that, but…" Sarah's expression seemed to be still trying to find the good in the new living situation, so I drove in another nail. "Not all professors get along. It's like not all lesbians want to fuck every woman they meet. It's not how it works. Besides, she teaches at a community college—"

"Careful, Lizzie. You're starting to sound like your mother," Sarah rebuked me gently, but she still knew it'd leave a mark, which was her purpose.

I glared at her, unable to mount a defense because I had none. Whenever my dead mother, who had been an unkind woman all of her life, entered a conversation, my brain shut down. Seemed like a good time to pop the Kiss into my mouth.

After several pregnant seconds, Sarah asked, "Do you want me to tell them we changed our minds?"

"They'll know it's because of me," I said around the bite of chocolate in my mouth.

"I'll tell them I'm having second thoughts." She splayed her fingers over her chest.

I forcefully swallowed. "They won't believe you, especially Maddie. I'm tired of always being the wet blanket in this family."

"You do it well, though." Sarah gave me her *cheer up* smile.

I put my headphones back in place.

Sarah moved closer and took them off. "Please don't shut me out."

"What else is there to talk about? You've been making all of these decisions knowing I wouldn't take to them. And, having Willow show up with her bags without any warning—" I gave a *what do you fucking expect* glare.

"I didn't know how to tell you."

"Clearly!"

She ran a finger up my forearm, her eyes blaring she'd been wrong.

I yanked it away. "No using sex to get me to see things your way."

"It's one of my most powerful weapons." Sarah flapped her long lashes, gazing upward and looking so damn sexy.

"It's manipulative." Not to mention it was working, but I tried hard to fight it. *Stay strong, Lizzie.*

"I know." She placed a hand over my heart. "It's also the best way to destress you."

I stared at her, my heart thudding in my chest, but my anger hadn't fizzled completely. "Concerning your mom. You could have at least sent a text when I was flying home. Just to let me know you considered my feelings enough to ask even if I wouldn't have received the message until I landed and well after you'd made the decision." I combed a hand through my hair, knocking my headphones completely off onto the pillow behind me. "I wouldn't have said no about Rose and Troy, and it would have prepared me some." From what Sarah had told me after dinner, before I disappeared to the bedroom, the night I'd been flying home, she'd woken at three in the morning and made the decision right then and there, sending a text to her mom but not me.

Sarah started to speak.

I poked a finger in the air, not wanting her to twist things. "Hell, even pulling me aside today and cautiously sharing the news about Maddie and Willow may have prevented how I'm feeling right now. I knew something was up when Maddie started to ask me for a favor when I was putting all the food away." Now I had a lightbulb moment. "That's why she was somewhat restrained during the shopping debacle when all the texts were blowing up my phone. I thought it odd she wasn't spewing out her typical zingers, but she was already doing her best to butter me up."

"It must have killed her." Sarah offered a tiny, cautious smile.

"Back to the kitchen, when Maddie was hemming and hawing, I thought she was trying to summon up the courage to make a reasonable request. Like cosigning a mortgage or along those lines. But to have her girlfriend —have they even reached that status since they met less than a month ago?" I continued to plow ahead. "Maddie doesn't have a great track record sticking to many things, aside from Demi." I groaned, smothering my eyes with the heels of my hands. "I foresee nothing but disaster, and sometimes I feel like I'm just waiting in line for your next directive. It's not a fun feeling." I sunk against the headboard, my arms folded tightly against my chest.

"In case you're wondering why I love you, this is one of the main reasons." Sarah traced a heart in the air with her index fingers and then placed one hand on my arms.

"My anger at you?" I yanked my arms away so she couldn't resume tickling them in the way I liked.

"Your passion about being angry with me."

"That makes zero sense." I pursed my lips, hugging my chest tighter.

"To you, no. To me, I love you more when you open up."

I wasn't having any of her explanation because even my body language was entrenching, not unfolding. "We just got rid of Ethan and his difficult family situation after his split with Lisa, which was uncomfortable at best, and now we're diving headfirst into the inevitable Maddie dyke drama. What happens when they decide they aren't actually soulmates or whatever cockamamie thing they've convinced themselves? All I can see is catastrophe." I mimed a blaring sign overhead. "Aren't you tired of upheaval in our lives? I'm exhausted."

"The problem right now isn't everyone else but the world. This plague has it out for all of us. The best thing we can do is band together and give it all we've got to survive."

"I am surviving by locking myself up in our bedroom and listening to an audiobook about fascism. It's how I relax!" I slammed a fist onto the mattress.

Sarah's smile showed she knew that, but she had a different idea in mind to help me recover from all the shocks of the day. She forced my right arm free and threaded my fingers with hers. "One thing I've learned about you and our family is we can get through anything if we all try together."

I knew she was right, and deep down I didn't begrudge her making decisions in the spur of the moment, but the introvert in me needed space, which was becoming increasingly hard with four kids. Now a mother-in-law, stepfather (on Sarah's side), Maddie, and this community-college professor with the ridiculous name.

But Sarah was staring deep into my eyes with a look of longing.

"Take off your shirt," I said.

"Why?" she teased.

"Because I need my happy place."

Sarah did, and I buried my face in her cleavage.

"I don't want to move from this spot until all of this is over," I mumbled, the warmth of her breasts spreading throughout my entire body.

## CHAPTER SIX

"Are you seriously going to keep your head in my cleavage?"

"Got a better idea?" I angled my head, so I could see into her eyes, my cheek still pressed against her breasts.

"I might be able to come up with something." Her smoldering eyes practically begged me to kiss her.

I moved my mouth closer but didn't claim her lips.

"What's wrong?" she whispered.

"I'm still pissed."

"I know."

"I don't want you to think one roll in the hay is going to fix everything."

She cupped my cheeks. "Please. I've been married to you long enough to know you don't let grudges go so easily, if ever."

"How do we meet in the middle?"

"Not sure you noticed, but I'm trying to seduce you." She shook her boobs.

"If that's your definition of middle ground, I could get on board." I failed at curbing a smile.

"You and your definitions. Can you trust that I didn't mean to upset—?"

"Are you fucking serious?"

"Let me finish, please." She placed a finger to my lips. "I knew it would, but it wasn't like I was intentionally making decisions solely to piss you off. You have to know that deep down."

"I don't like having people around all the time."

"I know, sweetie. I'm so sorry. Blame the pandemic."

Her eyes kicked it up into a higher gear, and it was becoming increasingly more difficult not to succumb to her wiles.

"Kiss me, please. I missed you so much," she said.

Our mouths met, the kiss starting off gentle, as if feeling our way back to the other. Sarah deepened it, ripping a moan from me.

"That's better." Sarah lifted my shirt over my head.

"I still want it known this argument isn't over."

"Again, I already know that."

Sarah moved on top of me, her breasts pressing into my bare skin, triggering every single nerve ending in my body.

"You do this on purpose," I said.

"Can you be more specific?"

"Using sex to get me to be quiet."

"I thought we already covered that." She stared down into my eyes with a knowing look. "Besides, is that a complaint you're wanting to lodge right now?"

My finger circled a freckle on her left breast, close enough to her nipple that it started to rise. "It's not fair."

"I know. I'm a terrible human being."

My finger traveled to her other breast, and my mouth clamped around her nipple. Sarah raked her hand through my short hair.

I rolled her over and got to work on her pajama bottoms.

She didn't have on underwear, resulting with her thighs already shimmering with wetness.

The desire to taste her intensified.

Along with the need to be inside her.

A victorious grin appeared on her lips. "I take it you've decided to table your objection."

"For the moment." My mouth worked its way up her right leg, bypassing her pussy and roaming down the inside of her other leg.

Her heady scent called to me, my southern region flipping to high alert.

My tongue took a meandering path back upward, Sarah's hips arching, and her swollen clit demanding my attention.

With one finger, I separated her lips and entered, while my tongue flicked her clit.

Sarah's whimper was the definition of sexy.

Leaving my finger inside her, I moved up to kiss her on the mouth, letting out a moan when her muscles contracted around my finger. For several moments, we kissed passionately, all the while I moved in and out of her, the slapping sounds of her wetness increasing with need.

Sarah bit down on my bottom lip and then sunk her head deep into a pillow.

It was time to work my way back to satiate her need, briefly stopping at one nipple.

Then the other nub.

My mouth continued to explore as it dipped farther and farther down her torso.

I added another finger inside as my tongue landed on her clit, taking it into my mouth.

"Oh, Lizzie." She fisted my hair.

With each plunge of my fingers, she became wetter and her hip gyrations more urgent for a release.

My tongue circled her clit, my own pulsing.

Her breath hitched.

Her fingers dug into my scalp as if I needed this clue to know she was on the brink.

If I were cruel, I'd stop, but I could never do that. Not with her so close to orgasming.

Sarah's upper body bucked off the mattress, and she stifled a *fuck me* moan so as not to wake the entire house.

My fingers dove in deep.

She let out another whimper.

Her body shuddered.

I concentrated on her clit.

Her thighs started to tremble.

My fingers curled upward, while my tongue didn't let up.

The first wave crashed through her, her entire body shaking.

It seemed to last eons, but in reality, it was probably only seconds. A true shame in life, since these were the moments that should last forever.

Finally, Sarah fell back onto the mattress, her breathing heavy.

I settled on top of her, spent.

"Feeling a little less angry?" She ran a hand up and down my back.

"A little."

"Oh dear, it seems my work isn't done yet."

"What else is on your *make it up to me* agenda?"

"Why don't I show you?" She rolled me onto my back.

CHAPTER SEVEN

The next morning, I woke early to get Calvin up and let Sarah sleep in since I was feeling somewhat guilty about blowing up yesterday, even if I believed myself one hundred percent justified. Actually, I deemed myself to be 127.987 percent in the right. Without a doubt!

I mean, how would normal people react to their inner sanctum being invaded by someone named Willow Greene just because the world was shutting down and there was a deadly disease running rampant? It wasn't like I was in charge of the world and conjured the pandemic to keep Maddie from her new squeeze. None of this was my doing, so why was I being punished?

Sarah knew I wasn't normal (if there was such a thing!), so of course, I was going to blow up on a Lizzie scale and have a hard time adapting. Not that I would actually explode in front of most. Sarah tended to take the brunt of my Lizzieness. I would simmer like a proper Petrie so everyone within one hundred feet of me could sense my displeasure, causing them to tip toe around me, but those, such as Willow Greene, wouldn't truly know where she stood with me because telling her and possibly hurting her feelings was a bridge too far for me, Passive-Aggressive Lizzie.

Sarah saw things *so* differently from me. That was the problem with being head over heels with someone like her. She not only loved people but liked them and wanted her peeps to be close to her when scared. That made my mind spin. When threatened, it was best to pull up the drawbridge and ride it out, alone and safe.

There was no denying these were scary times. Another major difference between the two of us, Sarah wasn't the type to seek solace in history, uncovering examples of individuals who'd recovered from terrible events. No. She liked knowing she wasn't alone, when I, the introvert, needed space to dig into my studies of human resilience without actually interacting with people because they ruined everything, and when you needed them the most, they had a habit of letting you down.

The house was large, but it wasn't as big as our Colorado home. Probably a good thing, or Sarah would have flown out Ethan, Lisa, Casey, Dad, Helen, Allen, and possibly Gabe. The last one would have added a huge complication to our already thorny household dynamics, because not only was Gabe my stepbrother, but he was also Maddie's ex. I doubted Willow would like having him under the same roof.

Was that my solution?

Invite Gabe to drive Willow Greene out of my sanctuary?

It'd probably backfire and royally piss off Sarah, which would most definitely deny me naked time for months, if not years. She knew the power she held over me.

I needed to go back to the drawing board.

Before I finished changing Cal, Demi started to rouse, so I got her up as well.

By the time I made it to the kitchen, with a kid on each hip, I was in dire need of tea so I could start plotting how to survive this pandemic with all these people. I placed the kiddos in their high chairs, and when flipping around to take care of my caffeine deficiency, I spied something outside on the lawn.

Squinting, I made out a figure through the mist on the window. The low during the night had been in the teens. Who in their right mind would be outside this early?

Then I made out Willow.

That figured.

Upon further inspection, Maddie's hippy chick was doing some weird type of slow-moving kung fu, because clearly her name wasn't ridiculous enough. Furthermore, she simply had to be a morning person who did some oddball type of exercise to balance her chi or whatnot. Gawd, I despised pretentious people like her.

"This is going to be a long… I literally don't know how lengthy this torture will be," I said in a cheery voice to the kids as I patted both of their heads so they couldn't sense my true feelings. Camouflage was a necessary ingredient to parenting. Never let the kids see my fear. I'd had decades of practice.

Still, Cal gave me some serious side eye, which made me grin. "That's right, little dude. Keep it real." I put my fist out for a pound, but he didn't stoop to giving one back. "Such a good boy!"

Before getting back to the task at hand, I stopped to watch Willow again, trying to decipher her movements and speed, or lack of either. A snail could lap her three times. If snails had appendages and Petrie determination.

I'd recently learned Patricia Highsmith, author of *The Price of Salt*, was fond of snails, keeping them as pets. She had a habit of bringing them to dinner parties and would pull them from her purse so they could leave slimy trails on the table. Could I start doing that all the while convincing Sarah it wasn't in fact a way to run Willow from my home but a homage of sorts to the author of the story that had been turned into the movie *Carol*? It was one of Sarah's all-time favorites.

Momentarily, I'd convince myself I could pull it off,

but then reality sank in. Sarah had a way of knowing what I was up to no matter how hard I tried to obfuscate. It was annoying as hell, especially during difficult times when I really needed to pull the wool over her eyes to fight for my very survival.

Besides, Willow was probably the type who'd like pet snails, and the house was full enough. I didn't need to add oozy occupants to my problem.

While I filled the teakettle, I watched Willow move her right arm like she was praying and then do something with her left. I couldn't imagine going to the grocery store with her in tow. It'd take ages to get to the front door. Not that Sarah was going to let me go to the store, and she'd taken my Instacart privilege away, which shouldn't rankle because she was now in charge of it, freeing my time to deal with shit, but it still annoyed me because I hated messing shit up. Even after years of doing it. I knew I was smart, but I also knew every-day life confounded me, and I wasn't holding up my end of the marriage bargain. Another reason I got up early to take care of the kids. I could change diapers and prep a simple kid-friendly breakfast.

After prepping tea for me and oatmeal and banana slices for the kiddos, I sat at the table.

Willow barged through the door, her cheeks rosy from the cold, not the exertion; that was for sure. "Good morning, Lizzie, Calvin, and Demi!" she sang in an obnoxiously loud, jolly voice.

Was her intent to wake up the entire neighborhood, not solely the household?

"Morning." My voice was gruff from not having my first sip of Earl Grey yet since it was scorching hot given the steam swirling from the mug.

"Do you do Tai Chi?" She squirted water in her mouth from what looked like an overpriced water bottle.

So that was what the *exercise* was called.

"Nope." I spooned oatmeal into Demi's mouth.

"Is that organic?" She pointed to the bowl.

I wanted to lie, to avoid the potential of experiencing a bonding moment, but confessed, "Yes. Sarah's—" I stopped myself from saying *a Nazi about it*, since I was constantly lecturing my students not to use the term as a way of normalizing it. I settled on, "She's into healthy stuff."

"Isn't everyone?" Willow refilled her bottle with water from the Brita container in the fridge.

"Good morning!" Sarah sounded way more easygoing than normal at this time of day.

"Are the twins still sleeping?" I asked, placing oatmeal into Calvin's mouth.

"Hopefully for another hour." She crossed her fingers on both hands. "Tea, Lizzie?"

"Got some, thanks."

"What about you, Willow? Would you like tea or coffee?" Sarah asked.

"I still need to unpack my special stuff. I'm very

particular about everything." Her voice matched her grave expression as if the survival of the world depended on her beverage choice.

Yeah, I'd pegged her as the worst guest at any dinner party. I wasn't the best since I hated most veggies or anything fancy, but that was easy to overcome by making mac and cheese or something like that.

I didn't think it would be that simple to appease Willow and wondered what it'd be like to hear her order in a restaurant. "I'll have the super green salad, but only if everything is organic and has fallen to the wayside on their own accord, instead of being plucked, and placed into individual slots on a plate made by happy monks with only sustainable materials that can be reused for eons until we all move to Mars."

I was all for being environmental but had reasonable expectations.

"Okay!" Sarah trilled. Was she overcompensating to balance the grumpiness oozing out of my pores?

If the lockdown went on for weeks, I was fairly confident my irritability would far outlast Sarah's perkiness.

I gave Sarah a *bring it* look, and she stuck her tongue out at me, more proof I'd won this battle. I made a checkmark in the air, and she shook her head, giving me that *tread carefully* glare she'd mastered since marrying me.

Not that Willow had noticed. It was like she

pooped out sunshine every time her buttocks graced the porcelain throne. I had to wonder if it was exhausting to stay so upbeat every second of the day. It couldn't be good, mentally. Sometimes it was absolutely imperative to let out your inner grump, although I probably gave into that need more than was necessary. Not that I would admit that out loud.

The tune of "Twinkle Twinkle Little Star" assaulted my ears, and this time Sarah used her pep to preempt me from growling, "No whistling so bloody early, Troy!"

"Isn't this great!" Sarah beamed, pressing her palms together. Or was she telling me she'd squeeze the life out of me if I contradicted her?

Willow echoed the sentiment, making a peace sign, and I secretly prayed she'd gouge an eye out. Troy, blissfully unaware of my mood, grinned as he stretched his arms overhead, yanking his shirt upward and exposing some hair on his stomach. I really didn't need to see that ever and not so early in the day.

"Who wants coffee? I know Mom will." Sarah, the obedient server in our house, pretended to take note on a pad.

"Maddie, too," Willow said. "I haven't converted her yet to my magical brew, but I'm working on it."

It was probably that mushroom shit that tasted like dirt and claimed to have lion's mane something or other, which only confused the heck out of me, because I thought they wanted to have sustainable ingredients, and lions were going extinct.

"I think it's only you and Lizzie who aren't traditional coffee drinkers," Sarah said pointedly, as if trying to cement a bond between us, the thing I would absolutely fight to the bitter end.

I tucked my head down, refusing to make eye contact with anyone.

Willow, not taking the hint, rested a hand on my shoulder. "It's you and me against the heathens."

I spooned in another bite of food for Demi, biting my inner cheeks so hard I was surprised a trickle of blood didn't ooze down my throat, choking me and putting me out of my misery.

Sarah took over with the kids, allowing me to bolt my tea, which had reached the right temperature. Then, I refilled my tea and disappeared into the basement in search of a folding camp chair. It turned out to be much harder to find.

"Whatcha doing?" Sarah asked.

I spun around in the cramped space. "Don't sneak up on me like that!"

"I came down the stairs. How else am I supposed to come to the basement for more oatmeal?" She pointed to the metal shelves housing all the extra food I'd purchased the day before.

"Looking for my red chair," I finally answered her question, my eyes continuing to seek it out.

"What red chair?"

"The one I used to keep in my car for spontaneous camping trips back when I was *single*." I stressed the last word.

"Sitting in the woods for a couple of hours reading a book doesn't equate to camping, dear." She patted my cheek like I was one of the kids.

"It does for someone who loathes being dirty and requires hot showers before bed. Do you know where it is? I can't seem to find anything of mine since the move. I'm still missing a box of books. Utterly convinced of that." I flourished my neck to punctuate the sentence.

"That's because I'm pure evil, and I've plotted every possible way to ruin your life, including having the movers toss one of your boxes of books in the middle of Iowa."

I pointed to the ceiling, which was right below the kitchen. "Bravo, because this is coming together probably even better than you thought."

"I have to admit I hadn't factored in the pandemic, but it really is pulling its weight in my *destroy Lizzie* project." She crossed her arms and leaned against one of the support beams in the semi-finished basement.

I stuck a palm in the air. "Don't even start on how you think I'm overreacting to everything."

"I wouldn't dream of it," she said with sweetness in her voice, annoying me.

I continued, even though Sarah was giving me her most supportive face because she was the loving type.

"I don't deal well with change. I need a lot of time for transitions. Even moving from the bedroom to the bathroom takes mental preparation for me."

"I'm aware, which is why I'm not giving you a Sarah lecture, as you like to say."

"How much time do I have left before you do?" I rocked back onto my heels.

"Three days."

My eyes widened, and I palmed the top of my head with both hands. "That's not enough!"

"It is. Clock is starting now." She kissed my cheek, grabbed the oatmeal container from a shelf, and went upstairs.

I spied a patch of red behind a stack of boxes and started moving them, nearly screaming with joy when I freed the chair. I managed to get back upstairs without anyone seeing me, and I made a beeline for our bedroom, more specifically the walk-in closet. I shut the door behind me, spread out my camp chair, and sat in the enclosed space, closing my eyes to enjoy the silence, occasionally sipping my tea, letting the caffeine course through me to give me the energy to get through day one of hell.

## CHAPTER EIGHT

An hour later, after carefully listening with my ear pressed to the closet door to ensure no one was on the other side, I slowly emerged from my cave. Unfortunately, before I could make it out of the bedroom, after stopping to take care of business in the bathroom, Willow crashed into the room.

"Hey there!" she said cheerily as she zoomed past me heading right into the bathroom.

I blinked at the shut door.

Dashing down the stairs, I located Sarah in the kitchen and whispered in her ear, "Willow is in our bathroom."

She whispered back, "I know."

"Why is she in our bathroom?" I pulled my head back to give me better access to examine every line in her traitorous face.

"She needed to shower before a meeting, and the other two were taken."

"What meeting?" I glanced around the kitchen as if expecting a boardroom table to magically appear. "We're not really supposed to go out—there." I pointed to the window, meaning the real world.

"She has a Zoom call with her department."

"What's a Zoom?" This had to be a dream. The plague. Everyone under my roof. And, now Zoom. That couldn't be a real thing grown adults would take seriously. No, it sounded like something the children watched all the while chanting the word Zoom.

"Right. You're still on spring break for another day, but you better become acquainted with Zoom and our new reality. Pronto." She snapped her fingers.

"Why? I'm referring to the Zoom part. I get the pandemic aspect as much as someone can understand a new disease that hasn't been truly studied yet." I folded my arms over my chest. "It's been a couple of days since returning home, and I'm drowning in newness."

"I know, honey. I'm really sorry about… life." Sarah caressed my arm, but I tightened it against my chest.

"I don't do Zoom."

"You will because it's your future, or more aptly, your present."

I waved a hand, wanting to revisit the matter, since I still wasn't clear about Zoom, but I definitely understood the other situation. "I don't want anyone in our bathroom. Ever."

Sarah squeezed my arm, where her hand still lay. "She's not going to hurt anything."

"That's not the point!" I said much too heatedly, causing Rose, who just joined Maddie at the kitchen table, to turn her head to give Sarah a *poor you* look, before diving into a conversation with Maddie as if nothing was wrong with the world.

"What am I missing?" Sarah said softly.

"I just pooped because it's my bathroom, and I didn't think anyone, aside from you, would go in there."

"I'm pretty sure she won't mind, and it's not the first time this has happened in human history. People have been pooping for eons." Sarah did her best not to laugh, but her struggle to control it was becoming painfully visible.

"Not in my bathroom. It's my space." I balled up my fists, and a tear formed in my right eye. "She didn't have anything with her, aside from a change of clothes and a towel. Is she using my bath sponge and other stuff?"

"I doubt she'll use your sponge."

"But you don't know that for sure." I cringed. "I don't like people touching my stuff." I made slicing motions with both hands.

"Lizzie, honey." She placed a hand on each of my arms. "I know this is a major change for you, but…

can you try not to lose it on every aspect on the first full day of everyone living here? You're going to give yourself a coronary."

"Can people not go into my bathroom?" I countered.

"There are six adults, four kids, and three bathrooms, two of which only have bathing capabilities. You do the math." Sarah joined Maddie and Rose at the kitchen table as way of ending the conversation.

"You do the math," I mocked quietly to myself.

Maybe I should devise a bathroom schedule. Sarah conveniently forgot to factor in Calvin was less than a year old, so he didn't technically need a bathroom. The other three were in various stages of potty training, which involved their own toilet upstairs and a special toilet seat for kids in the bathroom downstairs that had been designated as the training one because they spent the majority of their awake hours on the main floor.

There had to be a way to solve this problem, so I retreated to my office, needing to diagram the battle plan on a blank wall. I wished, not for the first time, I still had my Revolutionary War soldiers (which my mom tossed because they weren't the right type of dolls for respectable girls) I had when I was a kid or the board game Risk. Those would aid me in my quest and help me relax.

CHAPTER NINE

Hours later, Sarah came into the office, where I was holed up with Freddie, who was constructing something with blocks, while I bobbed Calvin up and down on my knee.

"There are my handsome men." Sarah hunched down to hug the wobbly and gleeful Freddie heading right for her.

"Are you lumping me into that category?" I asked, taking in my plaid pajama pants, hoodie, and brown slippers.

Sarah shook her head. "Come on. We're having a family meeting."

"Why didn't you bring Ollie and Demi in here?" I leaned back in my red chair, which I had brought down from the closet so Sarah wouldn't start asking questions if she discovered it behind the shoe rack, my first hiding spot until my senses came to me. "We're cozy.

Right, Cal?"

Sarah smiled at Cal but beckoned me with a finger. "A different family meeting."

I didn't like the sound of that but got up, toting Calvin on my hip. "Are all moms buff?"

"It's a pleasant side effect from carrying kids all day long." Sarah clasped her hand with Freddie's.

In the dining room, Ollie and Demi were on the floor with some type of building project, and Fred made a beeline for it. That boy loved anything and everything construction-y. Rose held her arms out for me to transfer Cal, who was still in the snuggly stage. After moving here, he'd turned out to be the cuddliest out of the four, and I hoped that wouldn't change.

Sarah sat at the head of the table and folded her hands together. "Since we don't know how long this… situation will last, I think it'll be wise to come up with a chore chart."

I followed her hand wave to a whiteboard propped up on an easel, which was the kids but had obviously been commandeered for the so-called taskmaster chart since her usual clipboard apparently wasn't sufficient for so many adults. Another tick in the *too many people in the house* column. I tucked that data point away in my memory bank to whip it out at the right moment.

Sarah continued, "As you can see, we"—she motioned to Maddie and Rose—"have brainstormed the possible chores that will need to be done—"

My arm darted in the air, and I blurted out without

waiting to be called on, "It doesn't have cleaning Hank's litter box."

Sarah smiled at me, sitting up straighter. "You always clean his box."

"I know," I boasted, a broad smile breaking out.

"Besides, we can't expect our guests to clean up after our cat." Sarah used the tone that meant I should pipe down and let her finish.

"But—" I couldn't have stopped myself if I tried, and I wasn't in the trying mood. "You said this was a family meeting. What's your definition of family?"

"Do you want help cleaning—"

"No," I cut off Troy. "I don't mind. My point is, if it's not there, I don't get credit."

Sarah nodded, her deep sigh showing she understood my concern, or at least knew I wouldn't back down.

Maddie snickered, much to my annoyance, but anything she did these days would piss me off considering she'd ambushed me with Willow, making Maddie another traitor in the mix.

"Okay, I'll fix it." Sarah stood, uncapped a marker, and made the addition.

"It only has one column. I clean it several times a day." I crossed my arms. If Sarah was going to make my life hell, why couldn't I return the favor? True, it was best not to antagonize her too much, because I enjoyed our naked time together, but we'd had sex the previous night, and since having kids, that was pretty much the quota for the week, so I felt safe enough in the moment. She could hold a grudge but never for longer than a week because she didn't have the Petrie asshole gene. "So... three columns?" I pressed.

Sarah wheeled about but obviously went to great lengths to rein in her anger before speaking. "This is only a template. Maddie will input it into a computer program, which will allow more flexibility."

I looked at Maddie. "I do it at least three times a day."

Maddie tapped her temple. "Locking that in."

I didn't trust her, so I tapped my own temple. "Making a mental note to remind you."

"I think the correct word is nag." Maddie painted on a not-so-sweet smile.

Rose paid no one any attention, aside from making cooing sounds to Calvin, who gave her some serious shade in his adorable way that accomplished the opposite of the intended look since it only made most want to hold him even tighter. Although he didn't fight being cuddled, I still wanted to say, "Attaboy!" This family could use another grump because I was going to need backup.

I looked over the chart again. "It doesn't have walk Gandhi. Fred and I do that every day." I glanced to our oldest son, who beamed a proud smile before turning his attention back to the construction project.

Sarah nodded but motioned she'd make the adjustment later and continued her spiel, emphasizing that all of us needed to pitch in to avoid sore feelings.

"I don't need credit," Willow said.

I leaned forward in my chair to make eye contact with her, glomming onto hope that her not wanting to lift a finger would be a solid reason to boot her out of Sarah's Pandemic Family Experiment. "Do you not plan on pitching in? I think it's—"

"Oh, I will. Happily. I just think checking off the chores as we do them is sufficient without writing down who does them. Recognition isn't really necessary. I certainly don't need it." She shrugged as if it were no big deal, nearly making me blow my stack.

Of course, the Miss Slo-mo Tai Chi and no regular-coffee chick didn't want validation. She probably firmly believed all participants in a race deserved medals no matter where they placed, including last. One word: pathetic!

The more I mulled it over, though, another thought hit me.

"Wait," I said, liking a part of Willow's insinuation. "Are we using stickers like we do for the kids?"

"We can," Sarah said through gritted teeth. I suspected she regretted inviting me to this family meeting, and quite possibly, it was my last.

I mentally added that to my victory column.

"It works for my students," Troy helpfully tossed in, and I wanted to give the man a hug.

"Lizzie, do you want good-girl stickers?" Maddie

teased, her blonde hair jouncing in such a way it felt like each strand was mocking me.

"We should call them good-human stickers," Willow countered.

I really wish I had a date affixed in my head for a countdown for when I could pack her bags and drive her home since she didn't have a car, one of the reasons why she had to move in. What kind of grown woman didn't have her own set of wheels? Or was that said to guilt me into saying yes, but secretly she had a vehicle tucked away some place?

"What about fun events?" Willow said, clearly done with the chores part of the powwow, even though the *walking the dog* aspect hadn't been entirely resolved, making me very uncomfortable in all caps.

On second thought, if we continued discussing things that needed doing, I might end up with more on my plate.

*Be careful, Lizzie.*

"What do you mean?" Maddie swiveled in her seat to Willow.

"We're going to be stuck inside for who knows how long. We might want to assign a person to come up with some type of entertainment for one night a week."

"Like a cruise director?" Sarah had a pinched face, the one that screamed it was brimming with possibility, much to my dread.

I'd barely recovered from that one time I played

charades on Christmas, the one where Sarah invited our entire family, and Peter ended up getting arrested. Not because he was that bad at the game but for financial shenanigans.

"Yeah!" Willow said in her hippy-dippy voice. How did her students take her seriously?

"I call puzzle night," Troy said. "I love jigsaw puzzles."

Sarah clicked her pen and wrote that down on a clipboard that seemed to materialize out of nowhere, making this whole new reality much more real. When she wielded a clipboard, there was no reasoning with the woman.

"I call game night." Maddie punched the air, her sapphire eyes sparkling with the potential of torturing me during the entire duration of the quarantine.

My insides turned to icy sludge.

I didn't know what I'd done in a previous life to merit my new reality, but I must have been worse than Attila the Hun, Hitler, Stalin, and Mao all rolled into one.

"I'd like to learn how to cook. I'll look into lessons for all of us," Willow said.

Rose, Maddie, and Sarah all said in unison, "Not Lizzie."

I smiled, since it seemed I'd get one night away from forced family fun, and I was using the terms *family* and *fun* loosely.

"Why not?" Willow asked.

"There have been a few incidents involving replacing the kitchen." Sarah bumped her knee against mine under the table, but I pulled out of her target range.

"Hey now." I raised a hand and scooted back into my chair. "You're making it sound way worse than it was. We never had to replace the whole kitchen. Just the oven that one time and then the microwave in a separate incident. I really don't think I can be blamed for the toaster. It was old and on its last leg." My defense lacked panache and made it seem like I was really that incompetent in the kitchen department, which had me torn. I absolutely despised having the stink of failure clinging to me, but I also didn't want to be involved in cooking lessons. Most especially with Willow the Interloper.

"But... she needs to take part." Willow wasn't so willing to let the matter drop even with the knowledge that destruction or fire was a possibility. I had to give her credit for being intrepid. Or stupid. A fine line between the two. She continued to litigate her case. "It's the whole point of family nights."

"You guys can do it when I'm teaching my night class. From the emails I read, I'll be lecturing online." I crossed my arms defensively, seeing if Willow could counter that argument.

She slouched down into her chair.

Sarah's pen clicked, and cooking night was locked and loaded without me.

*Progress!*

"I've always wanted to learn how to crochet," Rose said.

I had to admit I never associated the shopping fiend with crocheting. While she was of a certain age that didn't entertain a lot of sudden movements, as her roundness testified to, she was more the type to purchase frilly pillows to decorate the house, not make them herself.

"My hands shake," I said in hopes of wiggling out of another night.

"It can be a craft night." Sarah jotted it down. "Also, I would like to paint one night a week."

"Doesn't that fall into Rose's craft night?" I asked, scratching my head. I needed to shower but hadn't disinfected it after Willow used it. Would the others find it insulting if I ordered a hazmat suit to clean my bathroom if anyone other than Sarah or I used it?

"Kinda sorta, but I think two nights dedicated to the arts will broaden our minds." Sarah started writing the days at the top of a blank sheet of paper, slotting in the activities and who was in charge.

"Lizzie hasn't said what she wants to lead." Willow smiled at me, and I was sure she meant it to be warm and encouraging because that was her type.

That didn't change the fact that I wanted to toss

scalding hot tea in her face. Sadly, I didn't have any ammunition in front of me.

All eyes turned to me, most with sympathy, but Maddie wore an evil grin. "Lizzie isn't the type to join things willingly. Or lead."

"I do teach, you know." *Dammit, Lizzie. Why'd you say that?*

"Okay, tiger. Give us your idea." Maddie opened her intimidating eyes widely, daring me to take the bait.

"Well..." I rubbed my chin. "I like to learn things, so maybe documentaries or reading nights."

"I'm not taking quizzes," Maddie joked.

"Good, because I don't have time to write or grade them." I ground my teeth at her in all seriousness.

"Let's assign Lizzie documentary night." Sarah gave me *her nice try with the reading pitch*. "That's settled then. Every day is planned, except Sunday." Sarah set down her pen, a good sign that maybe this meeting was drawing to a close before I got into more hot water.

"Because that's the day we rest?" Maddie looked dubious.

"We may want some alone time," Sarah clarified, making a show of not looking in my direction but indicating with a slight jerk of the head that she was speaking on my behalf.

Only one night? I didn't count the night I taught, because while I enjoyed teaching, it did drain me.

Once again, my mind wandered to trying to figure

out how long this living experiment would last. The flu of 1918 lasted longer than a year, but surely, with modern medicine and a gazillion experts in this country and the world, we'd get a grip on it before the summer. Wouldn't we?

CHAPTER TEN

After the so-called family meeting, I got some work done, but when my alarm trilled, marking the end of my workday (Sarah had insisted on this alarm since I often got sucked into work and didn't notice the passage of time), I found Sarah, Rose, and Maddie with the kiddos, seeming to have some sort of conference.

Why did pandemic living involve so much dialogue?

"Anything I should be aware of?" I sat in a leather chair, putting my feet up on the ottoman, missing the one we'd left in Colorado. While this furniture was nearly an exact copy, it wasn't mine. I'd spent years getting the one back home to suit me to a T.

"Lots. Where should I begin?" Sarah chewed on her lower lip.

"Pick the easiest problem to solve." I adjusted in

the seat, but it still didn't give on my left side like I wanted.

"Music class."

"Oh, do I need to take—" That was when I zeroed in on the conundrum, and my eyes found Freddie, the drum-playing fiend. Ollie and Demi also partook in the classes but not with the same zeal.

"Exactly," Maddie said, adding milk to her coffee, which it seemed late in the day for, but I imagined the likes of Willow Greene exhausted all those around her.

I rubbed my chin.

Rose bounced Cal on her knee. At least he always had someone to love him, and from the peaceful look on his face, he was besotted with pandemic living. Sarah had been right about that aspect—the kids enjoying everyone under one roof.

"Huh… there has to be a solution," I said, my brain feeling like cement setting, not coming anywhere close to solving the problem.

Sarah snapped her fingers. "I'm going to make a call."

With my resourceful wife on the case, I took a moment to close my eyes, only to be jostled by Demi, who'd tugged on my pant leg. She darted her arms in the air, her way of saying she wanted to sit in my lap. Her reluctance not to speak on most occasions was a worry, but I wasn't sure what to do about it.

"You want a cuddle?" I asked Demi.

She nodded.

I was about to press her to use her words, but given the whole new reality, I decided not to stress out the poor child. I hoisted her onto my lap, her little arms wrapping around my neck.

Sarah waltzed into the room, her ear-to-ear grin announcing her triumph before she started speaking. "Bailey and Jorie are all set to teach the kiddos music class."

"How in the world will that happen?" I squinted one eye, wondering if Sarah had already booked their flights to have them move in with us. Just what the house was missing. More noise.

"They'll give the kiddos lessons over the internet."

I looked at our children. "Will that work? Do they have the attention span for that? I haven't taught many online classes yet, but I can say, from what I hear and the research I've done, it's not a cakewalk to keep students engaged."

"Maddie and I will be there."

Maddie mimed drumming, getting Fred to mimic her, followed by his precious giggle.

"Great job." Maddie fluffed the hair on top of his head.

"Mia is also zooming in." Sarah jotted something down on her clipboard.

Part of me had hoped during our move to Massachusetts Sarah's infamous clipboard would be lost in transit. It was possible I tucked it away in a box that was meant for storage, but it somehow magically reappeared. I suspected she'd simply purchased a new one, which was cheating in my mind.

"Oh, excellent thought. That way the kids can stay connected." Rose held Calvin up in the air, causing him to put his arms and legs out like he was trying to fly.

Demi tightened her grip on my neck. "Now that the kids' social lives are set—"

"That was only one of the problems dealing with the children," Sarah busted in.

"Right. Why wouldn't there be ninety-nine of them?"

Maddie leveled her eyes on me. "That's an interesting number. Any reason?"

"A hundred seems deadly." I shrugged. I hardly put much thought into actual numbers, but I enjoyed the expression people got when trying to analyze my odd use of percentages or whatever as if it held some secret clue into understanding how my brain worked. Good luck with that, because I sure in fuck didn't have a clue.

"School?"

"Mine or the kids?" Now I was bewildered.

"You and the university have solved your problem. The twins like going to preschool." Sarah's eyes fell to Freddie flipping through a book in his beanbag and Ollie coloring at the art table.

"But it's closed." I pointed out, not understanding where Sarah was going. "Are they doing Zoom?"

"No, which is why I brought it up. We have to teach them."

Demi had been watching our interaction carefully, which was why Sarah and I spoke in soft tones, ensuring we smiled even when it seemed disconcerting when matched with our words. It kinda did a mind-fuck on me.

"I can order some books—"

"That's always your solution." Maddie rolled her eyes, but her tone was encouraging since her need to be protective of Peter's daughter outweighed her desire to tease me.

"It's the teacher in me. Besides, books are my friends." I rocked Demi side to side, holding on. "Right, my little Demitasse. Books make the bestest of friends."

Fred took this as his cue to bring me the book he was leafing through to read to him. I placed Demi on one knee and Fred on the other and read *Yertle the Turtle*, one of our faves, effectively putting the rest of the conversation on hold for the moment, a good thing because the sensation of something pressing down on me was becoming hard to fight.

## CHAPTER ELEVEN

About a week later, Sarah, wearing garden gloves since we couldn't track down disposable ones, brought a box into the office.

I eyed it, nausea roiling in my stomach. "I remember a day when getting a package was exciting, not terrifying."

"Especially as kids, but now…" Her voice trailed off.

"Should we douse the box with bleach?"

"I think the gloves are sufficient for this part." She looked up at me. "Hopefully."

Setting it up on a table off to the side in my office, the one we'd designated as the mail spot, where one of us would use gloves to take care of the items, Sarah clumsily used the letter opener to slice the top of the box.

"It's the books for the kiddos." She took one out at

a time, wiping them down with disinfectant wipes. "Oh, this isn't—" Sarah held up a hardcover copy of *A Season of Splendor: The Court of Mrs. Astor in Gilded Age New York*. "Lizzie, why are you purchasing books on the Gilded Age."

"Is it from that time period?" I rubbed my chin before remembering I shouldn't touch my face. Squirting disinfectant on my hands, I still feigned innocence, not wanting to admit what I saw in Sarah's eyes. "Don't get that gotcha expression. I've been meaning to read it ever since Claire told you about Caroline Astor and Alva Vanderbilt way back in the day when life was normal. You remember it, don't you? The conversation spurred you to plan an elaborate tent party for the kiddos. I simply purchased a book. It seems like my interest didn't spur such a financial hit. Besides, what else do you expect me to do being stuck inside for who knows how long?"

Sarah shook her head, knowing I was doing some fancy tapdancing around my motive. "And it has nothing to do with the fact Willow is an expert on the Gilded Age."

"Nope. Not at all." I rifled through the books for the kids, avoiding Sarah's eye.

"Please tell me you don't plan on learning everything you possibly can about the time period so you can outshine Willow. You don't have to be perfect on every front."

"I'm doing no such thing. I simply want to be able

to hold my own in a conversation. This is me doing what you said." I circled a finger in the air over the book.

"So, you did know the book takes place during the Gilded Age?" Sarah yanked the gloves off and set them next to the box on the table.

Damn.

She tricked me.

Time for more tap dancing. "I'm simply showing an interest in Maddie's friend." I was still struggling to say such a ridiculous name out loud, and Sarah wasn't off the mark. Actually, she was dead right. I liked showing other historians I could dance circles around them. True, I usually did this within my own specialty, but it was good to expand one's interests, right?

"I meant you should ask her questions and let her talk, not read everything you can get your hands on and then quiz her in the hopes of getting her to misstate a fact or date. I see you do that enough when we're watching Nazi documentaries, but then you're shouting at the TV. Don't start quizzing her over dinner."

Seriously, how did Sarah suss out my master plan by simply seeing one book? Sometimes, it was a huge pain in the ass to have a wife who truly understood me, and I resolved to ensure I retrieved all packages from now on because I had five more books on order. Not to mention I signed up for The Great Courses, many podcasts, and had been cruising through other documentaries on my own during my private hour for exercise in the closet that none of them knew about. While I ran in place, I watched or listened to something to expand my knowledge. We had exercise equipment in the basement, but it would be impossible to hide my objective to kill two birds with one stone by exercising and becoming an expert on the Gilded Age.

I opened and closed my mouth, doing my best goldfish impression, unable to think of something plausible to get her off the scent. As it turned out, I was enjoying learning about the time period. Oh, I still wanted to show up the community-college professor, but I didn't want to stop my exploration either.

"Please, Lizzie. Give her a chance. Maddie really likes Willow, and I'm certain the feeling is mutual. Don't make things even weirder during these strange times."

"You're asking me to tamp down the part of me that's made me successful." I puffed out my bottom lip, looking like one of our kids after being told they couldn't have another cookie.

"By all means, improve your knowledge about your time period. I'm not discouraging you from that. Just don't try to humiliate a friend."

"F-friend!" I blew a raspberry. "I barely know her."

"She's living in our house. You have every opportunity to get to know her."

"Can I still read the book? It sounds good. I

promise not to mention anything in it to Willow." Damn! Why had I said that? I was pretty certain I wouldn't be able to keep the promise.

"Yes. And, you won't be able to hold the information inside."

*Seriously, how in the fuck did Sarah do that?*

She jabbed the air with a finger. "You're allowed to carry on a conversation. But under no circumstances are you allowed to lecture her." Sarah waggled the finger in a threatening manner. "Capisce!"

"Fine," I said through gritted teeth.

When she left the office, I stuck out my tongue. Then I took the book to my desk and got out a blank notebook and pen. Time to learn everything I could.

* * *

After an hour, I stopped, somewhat perplexed that I couldn't focus my brain any further on the book. Was I losing my edge? Simply getting older? Was all the fucking weirdness in the world sapping my mental powers?

Whatever the reason, it was time for a snack.

Opening the fridge, I selected some cheese cubes and grabbed an avocado, one of my new addictions. Years ago, I never would have touched an avocado, unless it was guac, but I was coming to like it on its own.

I pondered if I should scour the outside of the

avocado before slicing it in half so I could use a spoon to scoop out the bites. That was the only way I ate them and never understood those who carefully peeled the skin and then meticulously sliced the fruit into wedges piled just so. Sure, it looked pretty when done well, but I tried that once and ended up with a mangled mess that looked more like I'd slaughtered a dozen caterpillars, making it inedible.

"You and your snacks. We had lunch not so long ago." Maddie opened the cabinet next to the kitchen sink and grabbed a water glass, watching me wash the avocado. "Have you been waiting all this time to truly let your germ phobia out?"

"It's possible. Or, I don't want to die." My shrug meant take your pick because both were true.

She filled the glass with ice and then water from the fridge. Leaning against the counter, she said, "It's bizarre, isn't it? We have to make all these mental calculations about things we never gave a second's thought to before."

I finished washing the avocado and sliced it in half. "You want some? I was going to store the other half, but it always turns brown."

She nodded and took down two plates. "What kind of crackers do we have?"

"Club Crackers and some of Sarah's." I pointed to the cabinet, restraining myself from commenting that she'd given me shit about having a snack so soon after lunch. Part of me thought she'd tease me no matter what I was doing.

"You mean healthy?"

"Yep."

Maddie grabbed the Club Cracker box.

We sat side by side at the kitchen island.

"Why do you hate Willow?" Maddie placed cheese onto a cracker.

"I don't." I spooned in a bite of avocado, not looking in her direction.

"You don't talk to her."

"I don't know her." I prepared another spoonful.

"Talking to her would get you past that hurdle."

I sighed. "I'm struggling with having so many people in the house. It's not personal."

"You always had people over at your home in Colorado."

"Because Sarah insisted on inviting people over. I don't understand her need to surround herself with everyone."

"In her defense, she only invites close friends and family. Right now, she's doing her best to make everyone feel welcome and safe."

I turned my head to Maddie. "I'm not?"

"Safe, yes. That's innate in you. I know if anyone needs something from a store, you'll go because you wouldn't want anyone else to put themselves in danger. But welcoming…?"

"Rose and Troy seem happy."

"They're used to you."

"So, it's Willow who doesn't feel welcomed?" I scraped the inside of the avocado to get all the goodness out.

"Yes."

"Is this your way of getting me to try harder?" I sighed.

"Yes."

"Did Sarah ask you to talk to me? The one-two combo?" I mimed the boxing moves.

"Has she already given you the spiel?"

"When she found my book."

Maddie narrowed her eyes. "Do I even want to know what book?"

"Probably not." I set the empty avocado shell down on my plate. "I'll try, but I'm not good at small talk."

"She's a historian. She's one of you."

"Meaning?"

"Nerdy."

I rolled my eyes. "Everyone makes fun, but when shit hits the fan, people look to historians for references to make sense of their world. I've been asked on more and more podcasts to compare this administration to Mussolini and Hitler—"

"Willow would love to talk about that." Maddie hopped off the stool. "I would rather watch *Frozen* with the kids for the hundredth time."

CHAPTER TWELVE

A FEW WEEKS LATER, I EMERGED FROM MY office after my end-of-day alarm snapped me out of an audiobook about the home front during World War II. I rubbed my eyes since I'd forgotten to turn on the desk lamp in my office, and all the lights on the main level seemed to be on, nearly blinding me.

I waltzed into the kitchen for herbal tea but skidded to a stop. "It's Friday?"

Sarah was spreading out a tarp on the floor, the kitchen table shoved up against the wall to make room for the easels. "Why does it surprise you every Friday?"

Since painting Fridays started three weeks ago, I'd done my best to block out each experience. But that didn't seem like the right response to utter to Sarah, who loved this night of the week the most. As a substitute, I went with, "It's hard to keep track of the days now that we never leave the house and I basically live in the same outfit."

"Uh-huh." She wasn't buying it, but she was too consumed setting up the easels for our virtual painting party or torture, depending on which of us you asked.

I had to admit, though, Sarah and Maddie's completed masterpieces looked nice on our walls.

"What's the painting tonight?" I prayed for outlines of birds in the sky, because I could make black Ms against a blue background until the end of days. As a child, that had been my go-to during art class when I was a kid.

"Hydrangeas."

"Sounds hard." I added water to the new electric kettle and flipped it on.

"They're like little purple and blue blobs." She said it in a way that suggested she'd chosen this class based on the fact that I, her wife, didn't have an artistic bone in my body.

I hated that she wasn't wrong. Being the worst in any field annoyed the living shit out of me. Even Troy was better than I was.

The first week had been a beach scene with grass and a shoreline. Mine looked more like what would happen if an alien aircraft exploded over the ocean and was washed up on the shore. Somehow, when I mixed my paints, I created a green color that could only be described as neon-extraterrestrial guts.

The second painting involved bees and flowers.

Mine morphed into a mostly black design with sparing dabs of yellow, because when I'd mixed the paints, I focused more on black than anything and didn't have much else on my pallet.

"Maybe we should admit the truth. Not all of us have a flare for art." I plopped a tea bag into my mug. "I'm more than happy to read a book or something."

"It's not about the final product but the act of creating." Her tone said there was not a chance in hell I was getting out of painting night.

I poured hot water into my mug and sulked in the corner of the kitchen, because the rest of the space was covered with tarps.

Maddie breezed in wearing a painter's smock, her blond hair swept up into a messy bun. "I love Fridays!"

I let out a frustrated huff of air.

I think she was trying to give me her *you can do it* expression, but her pot-stirrer impulses couldn't hold back and she wound up looking constipated. To Sarah, Maddie announced, "I decanted the wine."

The local studio half a mile from our home had made a big splash in the fall by holding boozy painting classes. Sarah, Rose, and Maddie had attended a few, sparking Sarah's painting kick. When the pandemic hit, it took the studio a few weeks to get an online option up and going. Their plan, much to my irritation, was pretty brilliant. All Sarah had to do was go online, order enough kits for a certain painting, and then sign up for an hour to pick them up. The studio measured out all the paints and included brushes and canvases. They placed everything into bags and then set them outside for me to swing by and grab them.

The first time I went to get the kits, it was difficult not to lie and claim they hadn't been there. But innately I knew I'd be found out.

Not only did Sarah love the actual painting, but she really enjoyed supporting a local business during these difficult times. Every Friday night, they were guaranteed at least six adults taking part, but from the number of kits they prepared, I wasn't the only suffering spouse in the area.

Once, while I waited for a man to gather his kits, we made brief eye contact from afar, and the message was clear: *Not you too, you poor bastard*. Did every marriage have one bubbly person and one grump?

Soon enough, the clock ticked closer to eight, and we'd settled the kids into bed. Every single one fell asleep almost instantly, meaning my much wished for reprieve didn't materialize. Since the kids now had six adults taking shifts to keep them entertained, they were usually tuckered out by dinnertime and didn't put up much of a fuss when it came to bedtime. Not even Olivia squawked, which meant I was the only Petrie not pulling their shit together for the sake of Sarah's Pandemic Family experiment. Sure, the kids still had their meltdowns but nothing out of the ordinary.

It seemed to be only me, and I'd lost track of how

many minutes I'd wasted trying to concoct reasonable and totally unimpeachable excuses as to why I couldn't participate in *Adult Fun Time!* because it wasn't ever fun for me. Pure stress. Well, the puzzle and documentary nights were pretty easy to endure, aside from the griping about my viewing choices.

"Everyone ready?" Sarah asked, flipping her laptop open, instructing all of us to set up ours so we could follow along.

I made rapid movements with my right wrist. "Do you hear that clicking sound? That can't be good."

"Oh, poor you. Where's your brace?" Sarah narrowed her eyes, waiting for me to push to get out of painting.

I tapered my own eyes at her, but opened my laptop and picked up my brush, clasping it tightly. It wouldn't snap in half. I needed to work on my hand strength for that plan to pay off.

Maddie, eyeing my grip, gave me a *nice try* grin.

"Maybe you should look into dictation," Willow offered.

"How would that work?" I held my paintbrush up to my eyes, trying to figure out how to give it voice commands to spread the paint onto the canvas.

"For writing," Willow explained in the tone she used for me as if I was the slow kid in the group, reminding me of how my teachers had treated me from kindergarten all the way to my senior year.

"Oh. I don't think I could get used to giving punctuation commands."

"It does take getting used to, but it's freed me up to do stretches while I write." As if to give me inspiration, Willow bent over to touch her toes.

"I'm not bendy," was my lame retort.

Maddie snickered.

Sarah snapped her fingers. "Time to paint!"

I sighed and turned my attention to the lady on the laptop, adding white and yellow paint to my pallet like the woman was doing.

Forty-five minutes into it, we took a break, because the paint needed to dry.

"How's everyone doing?" Sarah refilled everyone's wineglasses except mine since I stopped drinking booze before the pandemic to control my nightmares. But could that be an excuse to get out of fun night? Become a fall-down, embarrassing drunk no one wanted to be around?

She studied my canvas, and her forced smile faltered somewhat. "Oh, I love what you're doing with the vase…"

It was supposed to be round, but mine was more of a mix of oval and rectangular, neither taking the lead, making it hard to figure out what it should actually be.

Willow popped up behind me. "Oh, yes. I see what you're going for. In fact…" She took my brush from my hand and then continued to add some streaks to my canvas. "There you go!"

While her addition did give my paint blob some more shape and dimension, I didn't appreciate her commandeering my brush like I needed help. I mean, I did need help, but I hadn't asked for it.

"I need to go to the bathroom." I set my things down to leave the room.

Willow went to Maddie's canvas and oohed and aahed over Maddie's creation. She was the best of the lot. Not surprising given her background in interior decorating. Sarah was in second place and Rose in third.

In the downstairs powder room, I yanked out my phone and texted two emojis to Sarah. It'd been brought to my attention that I didn't use emojis enough, so I'd been trying to brush up on my skills.

When I finished in the bathroom, I rejoined the group, and the class launched back into session, but I noticed Sarah's usually cheerful shoulders were a bit stiffer for the remainder of the night. Not to mention she polished off quite a bit more wine than normal.

It wasn't until we went to bed that she laid into me. "A death threat, really? I know painting isn't your favorite activity, but threatening the mother of your children? That's a step too far even for you."

I yanked my shirt over my head, carefully since not all the paint had dried. "What are you talking about? I didn't threaten anyone. Not even when Willow took my paintbrush from my hand." I held the hand in question in the air.

"You sent me a stop sign and then a bloody knife!"

"Yes!"

"How is that not a death threat?" Sarah folded her arms across her chest.

I groaned. "I meant if you don't get her to stop, I'm going to impale myself on a sword."

Sarah wiped her brow. "That's not how I took it."

"It's not my fault you don't understand simple images."

"Why didn't you include a noose? That would have conveyed your message a little better." She replaced her jeans with pajama bottoms.

"Why is it you can pick up on my meaning when I don't want you to, but when I need you to translate my Lizzieness, you don't. It's fucking annoying." I flicked my hands up.

"What do you mean when you don't want me to?" She stared daggers at me, holding her shirt in her hand, and it was hard not to focus on her exposed boobs.

"I didn't mean it that way. It's just..." I didn't know what I'd actually meant, so I simply stared her in the eyes, hoping she'd fill in the blank.

"It's a painting class, Lizzie. Why can't you try to have fun?" She put her top on, which caused mixed emotions. While I didn't want her tits hidden, it was easier for me to focus with them out of sight.

"There's nothing simple about painting hydrangeas. Why do we have to keep doing things I'm not good at?" I sat on the edge of the bed to remove my socks.

"It's not about what you end up with, but having fun and letting loose while you do it."

"I don't let loose!" I said in a heated voice.

"That's the problem! You're the issue!"

"I'm the problem?" I rested my hand on my chest.

"Everyone else is trying during this. Even the children. Why can't you at least try?"

"Clearly, I'm a terrible human being and not fit for society." Yes, I'd already known this to be the case, but that didn't mean I liked to have it thrown in my face.

"Not what I said." She stood her ground, her bare toes digging into the rug. Sarah had perfectly cute and round toes.

"It's what I heard."

"I know. You love to twist everything to be the victim. Why don't you text me a voodoo doll with a knife in its heart? You act like I'm torturing you by asking you to paint. By the way, how's your wrist?" She shrugged into a robe, which was odd since I thought we were getting ready for bed.

My forehead crumpled because the image she'd conjured in my head involved a dagger in the chest. Nothing to do with any of my appendages. "What about my wrist?"

She flourished her finger. "I knew the clicking in your wrist was a bunch of malarkey."

Shit!

I'd forgotten that excuse.

"Can we go to bed? Or are you not done lecturing me?"

"If I was truly lecturing you, you'd know it!" She left the bedroom, her robe flapping around her.

"I don't know what that means," I muttered to myself.

## CHAPTER THIRTEEN

"Am I an asshole?" I said as soon as Ethan answered my Skype call.

"I feel like this is a trick question." He painted on a sarcastic smile, his face unshaven, and upon closer inspection, I determined he was in the process of growing a beard, not solely sporting a moustache or goatee. How many men would resort to that during the pandemic? So far, Troy hadn't succumbed, but was it only a matter of time?

I briefly looked away from the camera to gather my thoughts. "I'm not enjoying having everyone here, and I think I'm the only one. The rest seem to be acting like it's a never-ending sleepover at Disneyland or something."

"Did you have any sleepovers when you were a kid?" He rested his chin on interlaced fingers.

"Nope." I made a clucking sound with my tongue.

"Because of your mom?"

"Partly. I also never saw the appeal. I like my space." I spread my arms to grip the sides of my office desk, which I had cleared aside from the laptop so I wouldn't get distracted while chatting with Ethan.

He nodded thoughtfully.

"This experience is showing me how different I am, even from those who claim to love me." I forced out a puff of air, but it didn't help me deal with the emotions swirling inside like an out-of-control blender. It was only a matter of time until my negative thoughts spewed out for all to hear. "Are you enjoying having everyone under your roof?"

"Well, it's me, Casey, Lisa, and Delores." He said the last name with ease, and it was that particular one that I'd hung my hope on that he'd see my point.

"Yeah, but..." I leaned closer to the screen. "Delores is your ex-wife's girlfriend, who was the other woman during your marriage."

"Yep, I'm aware." There wasn't a flicker of angst or anger on his face.

Fuck.

I was all alone.

Like I'd been during my childhood.

Perhaps I'd put too much hope Ethan would also be cracking from the pandemic. I mean, he had his issues with fluids, and I suspected he wasn't able to fulfill all of Lisa's needs. Did Delores save him on that front, and this was the solution to keep the family together for Casey's sake?

Even with all of these thought bubbles floating over my head, I had to ask, "It's going well?" I need to know if it was simply me who didn't want people close during times of emergency. Would I have been one of the assholes who wanted a dinghy all to myself when the Titanic was going down? I'd like to think I wouldn't be, but was this experience all that different?

"Sure is. We're all competing to see who can make the best sourdough." His eyes glimmered with competitiveness, but the playful kind, not the *take no prisoner* type I typically embraced with open arms.

"As in the bread?" I rubbed my chin, trying to keep my thoughts inside. Like who the fuck baked bread during a pandemic? Do something more productive. However, he could eat his creation, unlike my pathetic paintings that would be heading for the dump when I could haul them there.

"Yep. It has simple ingredients: Salt, water, and flour. But the process is so complicated." He stressed the word *so*, adding about ten Os. "It all comes down to the starter."

"I'm not following. Don't you toss the ingredients into a bread baker?" I wasn't simply confounded by the sourdough competition but the fact that Ethan was cool to have Lisa's new chick sleeping in Lisa's bed.

"We're doing it the old-fashioned way. No machines. You start with stone-ground flour and water, non-chlorinated." He made eye contact to make sure I was with him.

"What's hard about that?" I picked at a thread on my sleeve, twirling it around my finger, cutting off the circulation.

Ethan raised a finger as if saying, *patience grasshopper*. "Once you mix the two, it awakens the yeast and bacteria. The process discharges carbon dioxide and ethanol, causing a foam. It involves doggedness, and you have to feed it." He laughed, pointing at the screen. "You have no idea what I'm talking about."

"I don't understand why you'd want to feed or care for anything else. I'm overwhelmed by taking care of everyone here." I slumped down into my desk chair.

His expression changed to sympathy. "With sourdough, if it fails, you don't get tasty bread out of the process, so the high stakes involved are pride. Living with different branches of your family, the risk factor is extremely high, and from the look on your face, you're not doing well."

"I'm so tired of all the different activities each night. Painting is the worst night." I shifted in my seat to allow me to lean on my forearms.

"Why?"

"I'm the worst one. None of my paintings look anything like what it should."

"Tell everyone it's modern art, and they aren't supposed to know what it is." He laughed as if I was being a total goof and making things harder than they should be.

"I really thought you'd be on my side." I supported my forehead with my fingertips. "No one sees things like I do."

He slanted his head. "You're not talking about painting, are you?"

"Not really, I guess. My living situation is unbearable. I thought you'd be itching to toss Delores out on her ass, and you'd encourage me to do the same."

"I really don't advise you to toss out Sarah's mom. She may kill you." He laughed at his own joke.

But I needed clarification. "Which one? Sarah or Rose?"

"Both." He continued to chortle.

"I wasn't talking about them."

Understanding seemed to slam into his eyes, and he arched one brow. "Willow?"

"Yeah. Her." I pictured giving her the heave-ho but realized I'd need to up my hand weights to accomplish such a feat. It'd be worth it, though.

"Why don't you like her?" He seemed genuinely confused by this.

"I wouldn't say I don't like her, really. On the surface, she seems fine, a bit too hippy-dippy for me, but if we were colleagues, it'd be okay. I don't want her here. I don't like the idea that I have to take her under my wing simply because the world is falling apart. It's not fair I'm expected to." My voice was whinier than when the kids thought we were being completely unreasonable, and my eyes filled with tears.

"You don't, though." It looked as if he was choosing his words carefully. "She's a grown woman—"

"Exactly!"

Ethan motioned for me to let him finish. "It's not like it's really hurting you to let her stay. Maddie seems over the moon about her—"

"You two have been talking?" I sat up straighter, feeling foolish I hadn't factored that in before calling him to bitch about Maddie's chick. His opinion had been tainted before I got to him.

"Don't get your panties in a bunch, but yes."

"Why would that upset me?" It did, but I didn't want to admit that because there was no reason why it should. Maddie and Ethan had become close over the years. I wasn't the center of everything, even if everyone wanted to live in my house, forcing me to play that role.

"Because you'll start to think I'm betraying our friendship. Sometimes you live by the zero-sum game theory." He tossed out the words like they were so obvious, but I'd never thought of it that way. I simply wanted to finish first. Was that too much to ask?

His words made me feel as if I was being attacked, so I reacted Lizzie style, which means I completely overreacted. "I do not!"

"If you want my advice, play nice in the sandbox. This can't last forever, but you can do permanent damage by digging in."

"Why does it have to be my sandbox, though?" I tucked my hands into my armpits.

"From what I understand, she lives in a studio apartment. I think all of you going to her place would make your life even more hellish." He flashed that smile that challenged me to argue with his logic.

"But—"

"No buts. Not in this department. Suck it up, buttercup."

"I hate when people say that."

"I know. Usually because the other person is right, but you still want to charge ahead no matter the consequences. Slow your roll."

"Says the man feeding his yeast science project."

"Speaking of—"

"You gotta feed your new pet?" I sucked my lips into my mouth, not wanting his words of *suck it up, buttercup* to seep in. Why should I accept how things were? But if I didn't, the consequences would be devastating. Why did everything have to have such an impact?

"Yep. I've named her Sally."

"You named your sourdough starter? How will you eat Sally? It'll be like cannibalism."

"I love the way your brain works, Lizzie. I really do. To answer your question, I'll eat Sally hot from the oven with lots of butter. Yum!" He kissed his fingertips, making a loud smooching sound.

"Send me a video."

"Will do." He leaned closer to the camera. "Everything's going to be okay. Try going with the flow during all this. You can't save the world, but you can make it easier for those around you." He waved goodbye, and the screen went black.

"It's not, though," I said to no one in particular since everyone kept insisting everything would be okay when they were dead wrong.

Nothing good was going to come from all of this.

## CHAPTER FOURTEEN

Three days after the dustup with Sarah, when I'd been able to sufficiently mull over Ethan's words, I decided I should offer an olive branch because it must be hard for her, living with the likes of me. I found Sarah in the living room, sitting quietly with Calvin.

"Hey," I said as I eased into one of the wingbacks.

"Hey." Her greeting came out angry while mine sounded more defeated.

We'd been somewhat frosty to each other since my emoji fail during painting night.

I stretched out my legs, crossing my feet and extending my toes in my slippers. "So…"

She boosted one eyebrow in her annoyed and bossy way. Was it possible she was learning to hold a long-term grudge like I did? Even more ticks in the *suck it up, buttercup* column.

"Ethan told me I should apologize." He didn't actually say that with words, but I knew that was what he was getting at.

"You didn't think it was necessary before speaking with Ethan?" She slanted her head, and I couldn't decide if she was softening or hardening her stance.

"Uh... I didn't say that." I recrossed my feet. "This isn't going well."

"About on par for you. Apologies aren't really your thing. Probably because you don't ever think you have anything to apologize for."

*Ding, ding, ding!*

I didn't think I was at fault because she put me in the asshole box by having people invade my inner sanctum.

*Don't say that, Lizzie.*

I went with, "I've never been good at group activities. They make me uncomfortable."

"Why?" Her tone was softening, and Calvin stirred in her arms, but resettled.

"I hate doing things I'm not good at."

"You can't be good at everything."

"I know, which is why I usually stay in my lane." I added for clarification, "The history one."

"Just so you know, the activity is meant to be relaxing. Who cares how it turns out? It's not like we're going to try to sell the paintings or anything."

"But we could sell yours and Maddie's," I pouted, sinking deeper into the seat.

"Is that what's bothering you? I'm better at it than you?"

"Partly," I admitted.

"What's the other part?"

"I don't see the point in doing something I suck at." I tucked my feet under the chair.

"The only way you'll improve is by continuing to do it."

"For how long?" I snapped my head up to meet her eyes. "Longer than the pandemic?"

"Would that be such a terrible thing? I quite like it. When you aren't bitching, it helps me relax."

"But you can do it without me." I massaged my temples.

"Is that how you want things for us going forward? I do things I like, and you sit in your office all day, working on the one subject you excel at?" She displayed one finger in the air, and even though she didn't shake it menacingly, the way it stuck out did a lot of heavy lifting to her fear.

Yet, I couldn't help thinking this was a trick question, and I swallowed my first three yeses and willed my head not to nod.

Sarah continued, "It's not about who's better but us doing something together that doesn't involve work or the kids. I don't want us to grow old and realize we no longer have anything in common."

"We didn't have much in common when we got together." Okay. That didn't come out all that well. "I mean... you liked me then. Why don't you like me now?"

Sarah's head snapped back as if I'd punched her in the face. "You think I don't like you?"

"I'm not like anyone else in this house. That's becoming more apparent by the minute. I'm a stubborn curmudgeon who's resisting this experience with everything I have."

"That's very true." She was smiling like she meant it.

"So, I don't see why you'd want to stay with the likes of me. There are a million girls who'd go gaga if you even gave them a chance. I bet they'd paint every night of the week."

*I really was my own worst enemy.*

"Maybe curmudgeons are my type." She hefted a shoulder.

"If that was truly the case, you wouldn't be trying so hard to change me."

Sarah sighed. "That's not what I'm doing."

"It sure seems like it." I sniffed.

"I think you're just frustrated that you aren't getting your way all of the time."

"It's annoying," I said with too much meaning.

She rubbed her cheek against the top of Calvin's blond head. "How can we meet in the middle?"

"I can fill everyone's wineglass during painting class and then sit in the corner and read a book."

She shook her head.

I slouched even more in my chair, nearly slipping onto the floor. "When you said meet in the middle, you meant I should keep showing up to painting class and keep my mouth shut."

"Oh, you can continue to complain. I wouldn't want to take that joy from you."

"That's good. I don't know if I could curb it."

"I sincerely doubt it."

I stared at her, and she returned it.

"Are we done?" I asked.

"With the apology?" Amusement resided in the crinkles around her eyes.

"I guess so."

"Maybe we can find a class to improve your approach."

I stiffened in the chair. "No more classes! I can't handle any more."

"Deal." She looked way too pleased.

"You tricked me!" I wagged a finger.

She nodded. "It's pretty easy to do sometimes."

"It's not nice." I jutted out my bottom lip.

"Honey, even Winston Churchill liked to paint."

"Oh, that's a low blow. Trying to use history against me." I swallowed.

She chuckled and got to her feet. "Here, hold your son. I'm going to get started on dinner."

"Do you want help?"

"I'd love your company. I would like to point out I'm not forcing you to take cooking lessons with the rest of us, and you've been reading on craft night after you rush through whatever we have planned. Not once have I complained about that."

That was true, but I still needed to add, "As for the cooking class, you're afraid I'll burn down the house."

"True, but I know it's not something you'd like doing. I'm not that much of a hard-ass."

I smothered Calvin's exposed ear and made a face at her.

She laughed. "Can you give the painting classes more time? I really do think you'll start to like them. Besides, I picked out an upcoming design just for you. Keep trying, and don't let your pride get in the way." She opened the fridge and pulled out some ingredients. "I know you think you're terrible at it, but you're really improving. Sometimes, when you don't know I'm looking, I can see your face relaxing. It's good to see you let loose a little."

"It's not my natural state." I glanced away.

She cleared her throat and met my gaze when I trained mine on hers, concern flooding her face. "I know. That's what really worries me. I don't want you to get so worked up all of the time and have a stroke or heart attack. I want to live many more decades with you." She cupped my cheek. "I'm worried about you. Your shoulders are constantly slumped. You are not responsible for everything that happens under this roof." She said it in a way that made me wonder if Ethan had given her the heads-up about why I was upset about Willow, not merely her presence but the added pressure of taking care of another human being.

"Oh, good. I was looking for you." Maddie opened the fridge and grabbed a diet soda. Popping the top, she slurped it before continuing. "I think it'd be great for you and Willow to set up a history club of sorts."

Calvin fussed, so I eased him to my other shoulder. "What do you mean? For students?"

"Not exactly. She's been reading books about Nazis and has a ton of questions for you. What if you read some stuff about the Gilded Age, and then you two can talk about it?"

Sarah dumped frozen onions and peppers in a pan on the stovetop. "That sounds like a great idea. I'll ask Willow to suggest some books for me to buy to get you started." Glancing over her shoulder with a teasing smile, she added, "No more ordering mishaps for you."

I furrowed my brow, and it nearly killed me to hold in that I had been more than capable of ordering books on the subject without her finding out.

"What do you think?" Maddie asked me as she moved next to Sarah and started to slice the tomatoes on the cutting board without being told. The two of them had been making most of the meals together, and they didn't need to communicate when it came to cooking tasks.

"It's not the worst idea I've heard today," I confessed.

"That means she's excited," Sarah said.

"I'll need a brand-new notebook and pen," I spoke to Sarah.

She nodded. "I'll add it to the list."

"You have a ton of notebooks and pens." Maddie creased her forehead.

"It's part of her process when she takes on a new project," Sarah explained, and relief whooshed through me because she hadn't figured out I'd officially started the project weeks ago. I would never turn down the chance to get a new notebook and pen. I loved them.

I reached for my phone in my pocket. "Am I allowed to one-click books on Amazon? I don't think it's possible to purchase more than one copy of a book for my Kindle."

"I wouldn't want to take that privilege away, unless I have to." Sarah shook the spatula at me. "Don't make me use this."

Maddie burst into laughter, but I didn't understand why buying more than one ebook would result with being spanked with a spatula, so I gave her my confused face, which only spurred Maddie to continue laughing.

I stood up and placed Cal in his bouncy chair. "If you'll excuse me, I have some homework to tackle. Hopefully, you can get the new office stuff soon to really kick it into high gear."

"We might not see her until the next decade,"

Sarah said in a teasing voice, but I think she was pleased that I hadn't tossed cold water onto the idea.

In fact, I kinda liked it. One thing I missed about being a student was dipping my toes into different historical periods. When I was an undergrad, by the time I'd gotten all of my required courses out of the way, all of my electives were history classes. During several semesters, I took five to six different history classes.

Since I started teaching, I hadn't been super proactive about continuing to learn outside of my specialty. Maybe this would give me the impetus to change that. And, to show up Willow. Not that I would say that part out loud.

Also, I wouldn't have to go to great lengths to hide the fact that I was already engaged in Operation Gilded Age.

After dinner and completing one hour of puzzle night, which was one of the activities I enjoyed, I went to bed early. Or so I said.

Instead of falling asleep, I downloaded *Citizen Reporters* after exchanging a few texts with JJ. During our late-night text chats, I'd been learning a lot about reporting from the co-owner of *Matthews Daily Dish*. While JJ was sorta my boss, since I appeared on a TV show she hosted and produced, it never really felt like we were strictly boss/employee. She was one of the rare individuals I got along with, probably because she found all of my odd habits, like organizing my pens by the color of ink (each had their own cup on my desk, and please don't put a red one in the blue container because it makes my brain melt down), as charming and not overly anal-retentive. I liked being around people who didn't make me feel like a freak because, honestly, I thought that about myself enough. I didn't need it to be pointed out to me thank you very much.

When I asked to learn more about the history of newspapers, JJ had led me to Ida Tarbell and the rise of investigative journalism during the Gilded Age. It wasn't until I started my *school Willow on her specialty* project that I actually asked for a book about Tarbell. She suggested the one I was currently listening to and *Bully Pulpit*, which was next on my agenda.

An hour after my disappearing act, Sarah came into the bedroom. "I thought you were exhausted," she said in her knowing voice as she stripped off her jeans and sweater.

"I was. Of being around everyone." I paused my audiobook. Since it was only me in the room, I didn't have my headphones on because sometimes they made me feel claustrophobic, and my ears liked to be free.

Sarah gave me an understanding nod and climbed into bed behind me, only wearing her underwear and bra.

"Did I miss anything exciting?" I set my Kindle on my nightstand.

"Not unless you count Mom nodding off to sleep

on the couch." She snuggled closer to me, sniffing. "Did you take a bath?"

"Yeah. I used the new bubble bath. The lavender and chamomile one."

"How'd you take notes while in the tub?" She wrapped an arm around me as if saying *no hard feelings*.

"Oh, I listened to a novel. *The Age of Innocence* by Edith Wharton. Did you know she won a Pulitzer for it, and it was the first time a woman captured the prize?"

"I see your Gilded Age project is becoming all-consuming." She kissed the back of my neck, making my clit stand to attention.

"I would like to say Maddie suggested the project. I'm merely accepting the challenge." I scooted my body into hers as she continued paying attention to my neck. "I'm guessing by your seduction technique I'm not in too much trouble."

"Not at all. As long as you don't go overboard." Her hand slid under my shirt, moving up and down my back.

"I never go overboard."

Her laughter said, "Oh, please."

I reacted by climbing on top of her, rubbing my hip into her.

"At least the Gilded Age gets you hot." She stared up at me with her stunning, dark eyes.

I nuzzled my nose into the crook of her neck. "You have no idea."

"Is it the history aspect or the prospect of spending one-on-one time with Willow? She's very attractive."

I scrunched my nose. "You think so?"

Sarah nodded.

I gazed into her eyes and swiped some hair off her cheek. "Trust me when I say I don't have the hots for Willow. You—you're the one who drives me crazy. In the right way... well, in all ways. Even when you're annoyed with me. Your angry eyes are sexy as hell."

She laughed.

I leaned down and kissed her. "I like it when you come to bed hot to trot."

"Is that what you call it?"

I didn't answer, too busy focusing on her neck and then continuing my trek down south.

It wasn't simply the pandemic and having all the people under our roof that had transformed our sex lives into grab it while you can. Having four kids made it much harder to find the time for just us, but we did our best like tonight.

I made it past her stomach, her pelvis moving in ways that said her need was urgent. I eighty-sixed her panties and tasted her.

Sarah's back arched.

My mouth moved to her inner thigh, one of her most sensitive spots, and I loved the way she'd squirm and tap her feet. The gyration of her hips screamed she wanted me to get to the real work, so after one long lick from her knee to where her legs met, my mouth found her clit—wet and swollen.

Sarah's fingers grabbed my shoulders while I entered her. She let out a satisfied moan, her pelvis thrashing with need. It wasn't easy, but I loved the challenge of keeping my tongue in the right spot, and her breathing rapidly increased, showing she appreciated my efforts.

Her lower body was now bucking, smothering my face, making it difficult to breathe. I loved that I made Sarah this wet. Oh, so wet.

I increased the speed of my fingers, moving in and out of her, and Sarah's upper body lurched off the mattress when I hit the right spot inside, my tongue lapping her clit.

Her legs shook.

She cradled my head with both hands.

She tossed her head back.

And she came.

Hard.

"Don't ever think I find another woman more attractive than you."

She let out one of her *I've just been fucked* laughs. "It got you going, though."

I kissed her stomach. "Was that your plan before you came into the room?"

"Nope. It just hit me." She rolled me onto my back. "Sometimes, you're easy to play."

"Maybe I want you to think that."

"Is that right?" She unhooked her bra, making my eyes boggle. "You're such a boob girl."

"Another thing you have over Willow. No tits to speak of."

"How do you know?" She narrowed her eyes.

But I wasn't in the mood to be distracted. "Shut up and kiss me."

She did and more.

## CHAPTER FIFTEEN

A FEW DAYS LATER, I OPENED THE FRIDGE, but there weren't any English muffins. After hopping down to the basement, I realized the same could be said for the backup fridge. Even more upsetting, all of the cottage cheese was gone. Since the pandemic began, I'd been starting each day with an English muffin, a tiny bowl of cottage cheese, a fake sausage patty, and some fruit. Every single day for weeks. Once I got into a habit, it wasn't easy for me to snap out of it.

This morning, all I could scrounge up was a grapefruit and sausage patty, the original, not my preferred maple-flavored.

I stood by the toaster when Sarah breezed in, her robe fluttering around her. While I'd been eating the same breakfast, she'd been living in her robe, even now that it was warmer, although she'd switched to a lightweight one.

She took one look at me and asked, "What's wrong?"

"We're out of cottage cheese, English muffins, and this is the last, sad grapefruit." I glanced down at the pathetic thing on my plate.

"What are you toasting?" There was concern in her eyes as if I'd tossed in a living creature or something.

"Wheat bread," I said much too defensively. "I get sick when I don't eat bread in the morning."

"I know." She kissed my cheek.

"When I finish breakfast, I'll place another Instacart order." I scratched the back of my neck. "I don't like my new undershirts. They have tags."

"Why don't you let me handle Instacart, and come here so I can cut the tag out?" she said as cheerfully as possible.

I followed her order for the tag because it was driving me absolutely insane. "I know now not to amend Instacart orders, so I won't duplicate any of them."

There was a snip of the scissors, and I started to feel better. Only a little bit.

"I need some stuff, and it'll be easier for me to do it all at once." Sarah filled her coffee mug.

I removed the slice of wheat bread from the toaster and smeared butter on it. "Are you sure? If you give me the list, I can add it to my phone for future purchases. You do a lot around here. I'm not stupid enough to do it twice."

"Just to be safe, I'll take care of it. Besides, you have a podcast recording today." Sarah wore her *I'm so proud of you* smile, but I wasn't buying it since she wouldn't let me tackle a simple task.

"Fine, whatever!" I took a seat at the table with Rose and Maddie.

Willow was on kid duty in the front room, and Troy was presumably taking a shower to start a new day, but what was the point since they all blended together?

Maddie gave Sarah a sympathetic look and then asked, "Lizzie, what documentary do you have lined up for us next?" Maddie spooned in a bite of blueberry yogurt.

"We have two options. Birders or one about the *Portrait of Wally*." I bit into my toast, which was completely burnt on the bottom. "I think we need a new toaster."

Sarah sighed, setting her coffee on the kitchen table and taking a seat with us. "You need to get used to this one."

"I adjusted the temp again." I demonstrated cranking the gage all the way to the left.

"You either go for too light or way too dark. There's a middle ground." Sarah gave me her *I'm the wise one, so listen* shrug.

"Wars weren't won on the middle ground. Look at

World War I. Both sides dug into their trenches, and neither gained much ground." I dropped the too crispy bite back onto my plate.

"Making toast isn't warfare. Stop treating everything like it's a battle."

*Easy for you to say since you don't feel like everyone is invading your space and eating all your food.*

"I'm tired of everyone brushing off my reasoning because it doesn't make sense to them. Going back to my example, the aftermath of WWI led to German reparations, which resulted with the economy crashing, leading to the rise of Hitler."

Sarah studied me over the brim of her mug. "Are you saying not having your English muffins one morning will turn you into a dictator?"

"Stranger things have happened in history," I mumbled, once again annoyed that my fake sausage patty wasn't maple-flavored. Was it so hard for people to leave my things alone? Everyone knew which were mine and theirs. I know most in the house didn't let something like that throw off their entire day, but I was different. Apparently. I hadn't known I was such a delicate flower until Sarah's Pandemic Living Experiment.

Not wanting to focus on my pathetic excuse of a breakfast, I turned my attention to Maddie. "What time does Willow need my office today?" I tried not to sound whiney but failed.

"In thirty minutes."

My shoulders slumped.

"Hang in there, tiger. Be brave." Maddie tapped the bottom of her chin like that was supposed to have some impact on my mood or provide the strength I needed to endure a shitty breakfast.

Rose slanted her head. "I'm still confused about the documentary choices. Did you say herders?"

"No. Birders. It's about bird watchers in Central Park, New York." I spoke the words slowly and enunciated more than normal. During the few weeks we'd been trapped together, I'd learned Rose was losing her hearing, but no one seemed to want to tell her that. It wasn't like we could get her to a doctor right now, anyway. So, everyone else adjusted. That seemed to be the theme of pandemic living.

"That's different from the ones on the Nazis," Rose said.

"No one seemed to appreciate them." I took a sip of my tea to swallow down the rest of my thought that all of them were ingrates. That was becoming one of my favorite words to roll around in my head. "The one on the portrait does touch on the subject since the painting was stolen by Nazis, and it delves into the challenge of getting the art back to its rightful owner."

Maddie waggled her spoon at me. "We're living in a Nazi state—"

Sarah gave Maddie a mom look, and Maddie glanced away.

Rose asked, "What'd you say, dear? About birds?"

*Dear?*

Not only was she losing her hearing, but all of a sudden, she'd morphed into the old woman calling everyone dear and unable to follow the trajectory of a simple conversation.

Sarah cupped her hand over my left one and spoke in what I was now calling the Rose voice. "Lizzie has always wanted to learn more about birds."

"Why?" Maddie asked.

"I like them." I gave her my *duh* expression.

"You should get a parakeet. They're so cute." Maddie pretended to have a tiny bird on her finger, making cooing sounds.

Sarah laughed but stopped abruptly.

Maddie turned to her, waiting for the explanation behind the laughter or, better yet, the sudden stoppage. Probably because I'd kicked her in the shin under the table.

Sarah didn't comply right away.

"Well…?" Maddie crossed her arms. She wasn't going to let this drop.

Sarah gave me an *I'm sorry* smile before she quickly said, "Lizzie's terrified of birds."

"What, dear?" Rose cupped her ear.

Sarah basically shouted it.

Maddie and Rose turned to me, the latter asking, "Then why are we watching a documentary on them?"

"I like them from afar."

There was a scream, and I looked about expecting

to see an armed intruder searching for food. Instead, I saw Troy with a shaved head.

"I wasn't expecting that this morning," Maddie said, thumping a hand over her heart. "You look like Walter White."

"Or a neo-Nazi," I said.

"Why'd you do that?" Rose asked, her face pinched.

Troy ran a hand over it. "It was getting so long, and when I attached the blade to the razor, I misjudged, leaving some bald patches and others fluffy. I looked like I had the mange, so I…" He ran his hand over his shiny crown to finish his thought.

"Maybe you should wear a hat until it grows out," Sarah said in her helpful way that suggested you must wear a hat or you'll scare the children.

Troy nodded, heading for the stairs.

I grabbed my phone, which had given me the warning I needed to start crafting a lecture for next semester or I'd get off schedule. Pushing my chair away from the breakfast table in the nook, I said, "I have to attend to something upstairs."

"That means you have to poop." Maddie laughed.

I tucked my chin down and pretended I didn't hear her, heading to the bedroom.

After visiting the bathroom—and I totally hated Maddie knew that had been part of my reason for heading upstairs—I fired up my laptop. We'd crammed a tiny table in the corner for me to work when someone needed to use my office for official business. I had an email from Ethan and made a mental note to call him later, but I wasn't in the mood to hear how much he loved living with his new blended family. Besides, it was only seven in the morning in Colorado.

I did watch the clip he sent by a female comedian. The title of the YouTube segment was *How Hannah Gadsby's High-Functioning Autism Works*. Sarah and Maddie had mentioned the woman's name before, saying she was hilarious, and after the morning I'd endured, I clicked on the link to watch.

The bit involved a teacher trying to explain to a young Hannah about prepositions, which was going over the student's head. I had to admit I couldn't define them now, and I wasn't sure I ever could. By the time she'd reached the portion on the penguin eating a box, I was laughing aloud, and I had an *a-ha* moment because I finally understood prepositions. Go figure how an autistic woman telling a bit about English grammar finally taught me a rule I should have had down since elementary school. The world worked in funny ways.

Not wanting to dive into work right away, and in a much better mood, I scrolled through some online editions of the various newspapers I subscribed to, when an ad for a T-shirt caught my eye.

It read: *Nice Tits!*

Under that were depictions of different types of birds, such as Marsh tits, crested tits, and more.

Briefly, I considered not purchasing the shirt, but after seeing it on three more websites, I could no longer resist.

I selected my size, medium, and color, red. After entering my payment information, I got timed out. So, I went through the entire process again. Then again. Many more attempts failed, and I growled, more determined than ever.

"I won't be defeated by tits!" I hit the submit button and finally had success. "And Sarah thinks I can't manage ordering groceries. Wait until she sees my shirt!"

I did a little jig in my chair, determining that we'd watch the birders documentary after my shirt arrived.

Now, there really were no more excuses, so I started preparing the lecture on my carefully crafted production schedule, but every so often, my mind strayed back to the clip about the autistic woman and how I saw her logic so clearly.

CHAPTER SIXTEEN

THE FOLLOWING MORNING, I STOOD AT THE island in the kitchen, a sharp knife in my right hand, about to cut a newly delivered grapefruit in half, remembering at the last second, I hadn't washed it yet.

No one was in the kitchen, fortunately, or I wouldn't hear the end of it. Apparently, I was developing a reputation as the crazy, cooped up woman, who had meltdowns after small provocations. It wasn't an unfair characterization, in my humble opinion, since I was literally cooped up with too many people.

Me, the commitment-phobe couldn't find enough alone time, and all of my oddities were being challenged on every front. How was I not supposed to lose my shit if someone washed my T-shirts with sweatpants and towels? Who does that? I hate fluffy balls on my shirts, which was what happened. Never put T-shirts into the dryer with fuzz-causing items. Never.

I'd always had a way of doing things to help me keep my sanity. This experience was tipping me toward full-on cray cray with no chance of returning. Maybe it was only a matter of time due to my Petrie ancestry because no one could plausibly argue my family didn't have something wrong in our DNA.

I turned on the faucet, getting the water to scorching hot level, and squeezed soap onto the rind, even though I didn't plan on eating that portion because gross, but since the pandemic started, I'd been thoroughly washing everything.

Sarah wisely had talked me out of using bleach on food stuffs to avoid accidentally poisoning our children. Now that I thought about it, she didn't include our guests when mentioning her concern. Did that mean—no, she wouldn't even consider the possibility so I had to get that escape route out of my head. I couldn't bleach their food. Even if I could possibly get away with it by hiring the best legal team, saying I thought I was doing the right thing and the end result was simply tragic, not criminal. I doubted that would fly.

Even if the president had told people to drink it, which I would like to clarify I knew was wrong as soon as the words left his lips. I simply wanted to bleach everything that touched our skin and went into our mouths—which was the possible fatal flaw in my thinking. Sarah would have to lie for me on the stand. I couldn't ask that of her, and I'm not sure she would.

I started massaging the outside of the grapefruit with non-toxic soap, which was nearly the size of my head. The citrus, not the soap. There was a commotion in the front room, followed by laughter and then a slam of a door.

What was going on?

Had another *family* member shaved their head?

Did I really care to know?

I closed my eyes, getting lost in the one thing I could control. Cleaning my grapefruit.

"What are you doing?" Maddie asked.

"Sanitizing my breakfast." I kept my peepers squeezed shut.

"It looks like more than that is going on. The way you've got your eyes closed and the sense of calm on your face. Are you pretending you're feeling up a ginormous boob?"

With a *poof*, there went my happy, meditative thoughts. "Nope. Just pretending I was completely alone on a deserted island with no hope of rescue. Sounds heavenly."

Maddie had her head stuck in the fridge, scooting things around on the shelves. "What?"

"Nothing. I wasn't thinking of anything, especially not boobs." Maybe I should have said I was daydreaming about tits instead of imagining how I could get away with murder by bleach. Was thinking this way another tick in the cray-cray column? Should I bring it up with Sarah? No. That conversation would backfire and might land me back in therapy or worse.

"You're getting weirder. Do you have a fever?" Maddie took a step toward me and placed her hand on my forehead.

"Nope, I feel perfectly fine." Unfortunately. If I had symptoms, would everyone have to head to Rose's place? I pulled away from Maddie's hand, not wanting to be touched, and rinsed all the suds off my pink grapefruit.

"Sarah, you need to give Lizzie more special time with your girls, or she's going to replace you with grapefruit."

Sarah, who held up an empty coffee mug, gave Maddie a puzzled look but didn't take the bait. Maybe she sensed from my reddening face I wasn't in the mood for teasing. At the kitchen table, I sat down with my fruit, English muffin, maple-flavored fake sausage, and a small bowl of cottage cheese. At least I had my normal breakfast, and I tried focusing on the good.

"Where are the kids?" I asked Sarah.

"With Mom. They're reading a book about baby animals."

Fred waddled in, grinning.

"What's a baby swan called, Fred?" I smiled at him, tickled by how much he loved learning words, just like I did. I started to say *cygnet* but was cut off.

"Swastikas," Maddie quipped, causing Sarah to burst into laughter before she was able to rein it in.

Fred looked at Maddie and studied Sarah's reaction before repeating the word, causing Sarah's laughter dam to break.

I glared at Maddie. "Please, don't teach him anymore Nazi things."

Maddie feigned shock. "But you love the Nazis. Look at all your books in the office with swastikas on them." She spoke the word slowly for Fred to understand.

Fred turned to me but lost interest when Hank appeared from a potted tree off to the side, meowing and arching his back from a long nap.

"Someone's hungry," I said, getting up to get Hank fresh wet food.

"He's going to get fat if you keep feeding him every time he meows," Sarah said.

I looked at my watch. "It's breakfast time. I haven't fed him his wet food yet today. Have you?" I met her eyes and then Maddie's, both of them shaking their heads. "Do I—?"

"Yes, dear. I'll add *feed Hank* to the chart." Sarah pinched my cheek, a little too hard, on her way to the coffee pot.

"Don't forget Gandhi." The Yorkie popped up his head. "Have you added walking the dog? Last time I checked it wasn't on the chart. Speaking of, I'm eating late today, so I should do that right after everyone eats."

"Take Fred," she said, despite the fact that I always

took him as he was the only one of the four kids who enjoyed the experience.

It was Fred's turn to perk up, which was the true reason Sarah had said it. We always tried to make each child feel special and get time alone with us.

"Gladly," I said, giving Fred a conspiratorial smile, all the while doing my best not to mention getting another sticker but failing when I started to speak. "Have you decided on what type of new stickers we should get? I wasn't particularly fond of the stars." I let my voice trail off in my pathetic way, which usually resulted with the desired effect.

Sarah snorted. "No more ordering for you, or are you forgetting about the groceries?"

"Do they sell swastika stickers?" Maddie made eye contact with Fred.

I ignored Maddie but said to Sarah, "Are you ever going to forget about that? Besides, it could have happened to anyone." I held my grapefruit spoon in a threatening manner.

"Funny, but the only one I know of it happening to is you. I didn't have any issues with Instacart yesterday." Sarah crossed her arms.

"Didn't they have *good human* stickers?"

"I'll do it today. You're worse than the kids, sometimes. Who knows how many stickers you'd actually buy?"

"You can never have too many." I scrolled through options on my phone. "I added a magnetic Disney chore chart to the Amazon wish list in case you were curious about what I like." I put my phone down. "We might need one for each person. I can set up a command center in the finished part of the basement."

A pained expression crossed Sarah's face, but she said, "I promise to look at it soon, honey."

"Thank you." I opted not to crow about ordering my *Nice Tits* shirt, preferring to unveil it on the night we watched the birders documentary to prove I could order things without any mishaps.

Oddly, Freddie chirped like a bird, making me think, not for the first time, he had some form of ESP.

Sarah, oblivious to all my thoughts, smiled at our son. "Let's get your shoes and jacket on Fred."

He giggled and ran to the entryway.

Sarah got him ready while I finished eating. Parenthood had taught me to wolf down every meal or risk starvation.

In the entryway, I slipped on my lightweight coat, clipped Gandhi into the leash, and then held onto Fred's hand, giving it a squeeze, which he reciprocated, briefly staring up at me as if saying thanks for always making this time together.

Outside, the sun blared overhead, but it was still chilly given it was late May. The cold didn't seem to bother Fred, and he continued grinning, his cheeks turning pink. This was his element. Being outdoors walking his dog, because Gandhi had taken to him since the move.

"What do you think about all of this, Fred?"

He extended a hand. "Bird."

"It is a lovely bird."

Fred puffed out his chest.

"What color is it?"

"Red," he proudly stated.

"Correct. It's a red cardinal." I knew the red before cardinal was superfluous, but it was a teaching tool. Besides, I liked to say red cardinal. Sue me. "What else do you see?"

"Tree."

He continued to blurt out words, including car, fire hydrant, sidewalk, and truck—his favorite word these days. When he said man, I glanced up, spying a man heading toward us. Gripping Gandhi's lead, I stopped the terrier from bounding ahead. The man and I hesitated for a long second before he crossed the street with an apologetic flick of the hand. I repeated the gesture.

I wasn't typically a people person, and it wasn't all that unusual for me to go out of my way to avoid them. But since the start of the pandemic, I was terrified to walk by a man simply because he was a human being who could possibly have the virus. I wasn't worried about my own health, per se, but that of my loved ones.

How strange that simply seeing another person gave me the urge to sweep my son and dog into my arms and run back inside the safety of my house, barricading the doors. Even after all of these weeks. Would that impulse end when all this was said and done?

However, overreacting wasn't the right thing to do with my son by my side. After I controlled my heart rate and brain, I continued walking with Freddie. I didn't want to embed fear into his very being like my mother had with me from my birth. My goal was to foster his inquisitiveness, not scold him for seeking out knowledge.

Also, one of Fred's greatest joys was going for a walk with me and Gandhi twice a day so he could spot trucks and birds. It was such an innocent and pure delight we could do as mother and son: walking and pointing out things Fred liked to see and speak aloud. We'd seen other humans during this, but normally, by the time I spied someone, they were already on the other side of the street. Our neighborhood was taking the disease seriously, and I hadn't interacted with a human outside of my family, aside from Zoom, since I'd flown back from Colorado. If I was socially awkward before the pandemic, I feared this experience would only make it that much worse.

Luckily, Fred didn't seem to notice my anxiety, and he continued to spout out everything he saw: fence, several more birds, cat, and two more trucks (one technically was an SUV, but I hadn't taught him that one yet). He merrily chanted the word the final steps home.

"How'd it go?" Sarah asked.

"Weird," I whispered.

Fred chirped, "Truck."

Sarah leaned down and kissed the top of his head, where he preferred kisses these days, and he always presented his crown like a battering ram. "Grandma is making a snack in the kitchen."

Fred waddled toward the kitchen.

When it was just the two of us, Sarah asked, "Are you okay?"

I explained about the man and my fears. I buried my head into her chest while she made soothing sounds. "This is weird. So fucking weird and there's no end in sight."

CHAPTER SEVENTEEN

That afternoon, I was nearing the end of my kid duty shift. Calvin was taking a nap, and Freddie and Olivia had reached their max for painting, but Demi, who was turning out to be quite the little artist, was still hanging with me.

"Wow, my little Demitasse. Look at that." I compared her finger painting masterpiece to my own. "You can actually tell yours is the mountains. As for mine, it's more of a big blob."

"Blob!" she exclaimed with all the exuberance of a happy child without a care in the world.

"Yes. Mommy did a blob." For some reason, I didn't mind that Demi was a far superior creative when it came to finger painting. However, looking into her blue eyes, I saw my brother Peter, and I understood her life would never be easy. I could relate to that, having my own issues with my parents.

Demi shrieked with glee and placed both of her hands on my cheeks, smearing paint all over my face.

Maddie walked into the room and laughed. "You're a sight." She swept Demi up into her arms. "Let's get you cleaned up, little miss."

"What about me?" I dabbed my face with the front of my painting shirt, which had old paint from previous kid shifts embedded in the threads.

"I'm pretty sure you know how to work the shower." Maddie and Demi disappeared into the downstairs bathroom for a spot clean for the child.

I, on the other hand, needed to be presentable, and I bolted up the stairs heading for my shower, because I had thirty minutes before I had to hop on a call for JJ's show.

Sarah was in the bathroom, tugging her arms into a bathrobe after her own shower. "Who's with the kids?"

"Maddie has Demi. Troy is teaching Fred how to play 'Twinkle Twinkle Little Star' on the drums. Calvin is napping, and I think your mom has Ollie, but it's hard to keep track." I yanked my shirt carefully over my head, trying to avoid getting paint in my hair. I hated picking it out without tugging my scalp too much. "I have twenty minutes before I have to hop on a call to prep with the producer."

Sarah nodded, only half listening.

I cranked on the water to the shower, sticking my

hand under the stream and waiting for it to hit the right temperature. "You okay?"

She nodded again, not looking in my direction.

"You're not. What's wrong?"

Sarah tried to lift her lips into a smile, but it only got halfway before drooping. "With all this craziness and how hard it is to keep up with the kids, even with all the adults in the house, I don't think I'm going to start law school in the fall. Or ever."

I'd been wondering about that since she received two acceptance letters, given how everything on the planet had ground to a halt. "Are you sure? I know my department is getting creative with Zoom classes. Even when your mom and Troy aren't living with us anymore, they're not far away. Two of my students have their kids on their laps, and it's fine. Universities are practically begging for students right now. They'll work with you."

She started to speak but then said, "Let's discuss it later tonight over wine."

"I wish I could have some mommy juice before my call to relax some."

"It's only two in the afternoon, and you don't drink anymore." She laughed, looking as if she also wanted a glass. "Good luck on the call. Remember, Fred likes to leave for his afternoon walk right at three. Why'd you switch the time?"

My son got his punctuality from me. "Oh, I'm

aware, and I didn't make the adjustment; the show did."

Soon enough, I was downstairs, and my hair was mostly dry.

I flipped on the light Maddie had purchased for my appearances, placed my laptop on a pile of books for a better camera angle, hooked up my microphone, and shoved in my AirPods. By the time I was testing my microphone, Maddie popped in to apply a small amount of makeup. After a couple of disastrous appearances, Maddie had taken it upon herself to help me with my in-home studio and beautification.

"Ready for your close-up?" She held a pink makeup bag.

"You never get tired of that joke." I still smiled because I also liked it.

"Nothing seems to change much day to day, so why should I try harder?"

"That's the attitude!" I flashed a sarcastic thumbs-up.

She started to powder my face and spoke in a loud voice, "I talked to your dad this morning."

"How's he doing?" I reinserted my left AirPod, trying to get a better fit.

"He's frantically trying to get Peter out of jail to serve the rest of his sentence at home." Maddie puckered her lips as her way of saying for me to do that with my own, which I did, and she applied a soft pink lipstick, close to my natural color. It took weeks of intense back and forth for us to settle on this shade. ChapStick had been my only lip product for years before my TV gig.

After she put everything back into the bag, I said, "He'll figure it out. He always does."

Maddie's sparkling eyes blared with worry. "I hope so. You're all set. Happy nerding out!"

She left the room right when the producer got on the line.

I'd been doing the show for months now, and it'd simply become part of my routine. Soon enough, I was live.

As my portion started to wrap up, Fred came into the room, causing me to look up. I tried to wave for him to stay put, but he either didn't see or didn't care.

Instead, he climbed onto my lap.

JJ noticed him. "Oh, hey. It looks like we have a special guest today. How are you, Freddie?"

My face turning red, I pointed to the screen. "Say hi to JJ, Fred."

"Hi, JJ!" He waved.

"What do you have planned this afternoon?" JJ asked, showing how comfortable she was with kids even on a live show. She often had Mia on her lap during the planning calls for segments but never on air. At least, not when I was present.

"We're going to visit baby animals!"

Puzzled, I tilted my head. "We are? I thought we were going for a walk."

He nodded. "The book, Mommy."

"Oh!" I bonked my forehead, my other arm holding onto Fred. "We're reading about baby animals this week," I explained to the audience. "He loves animals."

"What's your favorite?" JJ asked.

"Swastikas!" Freddie blurted out with such glee.

Two other guests in their window boxes looked stunned, and I felt my throat constrict but was able to push out, "He means baby swans. Not swastikas."

Luckily, JJ picked up on my utter mortification and said, "We'll let you get to it, then. Thank you, Dr. Petrie. Bye, Freddie!" She waved enthusiastically as if to let him know he hadn't done anything wrong.

He waved goodbye to the television world, and I closed my laptop.

She didn't normally say my title and last name, but I think she was throwing me a bone.

Fred, completely oblivious to my unease, said, "Walk time, Mommy!"

I carried Freddie to the kitchen, and Sarah asked, "How was the call?"

"Freddie made a guest appearance and announced I was teaching him about swastikas." I glared at Maddie but ensured my voice didn't sound scold-y, not wanting to discourage Fred in any way from speaking his mind.

Maddie's eyes widened, and she smothered her mouth to keep the laughter inside.

"Oh dear!" was all Sarah could manage before she started laughing.

Freddie looked at Maddie and Sarah and chanted, "Swastikas!"

"Yes, Freddie. Mommy is a swastika expert." Maddie clapped her hands to keep the conversation light and fluffy.

I announced, "We're going for our walk now. Right, Freddie?"

"Walk!" He hopped up and down on one foot.

Sarah gave me a sympathetic look, but she was on her phone, no doubt searching for the YouTube clip that was certain to appear soon.

* * *

THAT NIGHT, SARAH AND I CUDDLED IN THE office after finishing the evening's forced family fun.

"You okay?" she asked.

I knew she was asking about Freddie's moment with fame. "He did look so cute and happy. If only my actual students had that level of interest in learning things."

"He's at the age when everything is exciting, and he takes after you in so many ways." She leaned into me.

"Socially awkward?"

She shoved her shoulder into mine and took a fortifying sip of her wine. "I was going for loves to learn new words."

"Right. That makes sense."

Sarah let out a cleansing breath. "This has been a day, hasn't it?"

"Did you want to talk about law school?"

She chewed on her bottom lip. "It doesn't seem worth it now. With everything going on. Not to mention, do I really need to take that on along with raising four kids?"

"Yes, because I know it's something you want. We have a lot of people to help out, including me. I mean, look at how I handled my TV appearance with Fred. He can add YouTube star to his resume." I laughed, because hours later, the memory was much more pleasing than the actual moment.

"He's got stiff competition since so many kids and pets are making uninvited cameos."

"I wish I'd had a snappier line when he said it."

"Like what?" Her eyes grew big.

"No idea. Let's face it; stand-up isn't in my future." Again, I thought back to the Hannah Gadsby clip, making a mental note to watch more.

"Sadly, no. We could use another income stream, though."

"We aren't that bad off. Let's get back to the law school thread. As in you going. You've been accepted."

She nodded. "True, which was a nice ego boost."

"That's not the reason you applied."

Sarah rested her head against the back of the couch. "Look at today. Maddie and Mom were watching Fred, and he still got into your office while recording."

"Yep, and news flash, I survived."

"Your face was beet red." She tugged on her shirt collar, and I wondered if it was out of sympathy or if the wine was making her flush.

"Oh, I think I can still feel the burn." I ran a hand over my cheek. "It happened. It might happen with a different kid next time or with one of the pets. The thing is everyone is adjusting to working from home. There are some speed bumps, but we have to keep going. I think the same is true for you and going back to school. You can defer, right? Not that I'm saying you should."

"Yes, but I'll be a year older." Her shoulders sagged.

"We all will be."

"When should I simply accept I won't be a lawyer? Why did I ever think I could start a new career at my age?"

"You should never accept that. Especially not before you even try."

"I did try! I took the LSAT. Got in," she said in a tone that implied that was all she needed, but the disappointment in her eyes was palpable.

"Of which I'm very proud. Now for the next step,

either this fall or the following term, you're going." I made a definitive wave of the hand.

"You're not the boss of me."

"In this regard, I am." I took a sip of my sparkling water. "Glad that's settled."

"I'll be one of the oldest students," she said barely above a whisper.

"I don't know about that, but you'll be the sexiest."

"I have four kids."

"Don't forget the pets." I raised two fingers in the air.

"I didn't give birth to them."

"No, but they're still an important part of this family." I yawned.

She shook her head. "Oh, no. You can't get me hot and bothered by laying down the law and then want to go to sleep."

I feigned not understanding. "It's bedtime."

"For everyone else. Not us." She batted her lashes at me.

"Is everyone asleep?" It was weird for me, having so many people who could potentially hear things I'd rather they didn't.

"I put sleeping pills in their broccoli."

"Is that right? Another reason never to eat my veggies."

"Shut up and take me to bed."

CHAPTER EIGHTEEN

When we retreated to our bedroom, as soon as Sarah clicked the door shut, I was unable to hold back a yawn.

"No way. You're not getting out of this." Sarah shook a finger. "Sometimes, it's the only thing keeping me sane during all of this. I love my Mom, Troy, and Maddie, but…" She left the rest unsaid.

I thought it best not to add my two cents about Troy whistling the same tune or having to shout for Rose to hear something. And, no way was I going to dip my toes into the Willow waters.

But I couldn't think of something plausible to say, so I resorted to, "Out of what?" knowing she meant sex. I wasn't that clueless, just too tired to tax my brain.

"Nice try. I can see many of your thoughts flitting

through your mind. It's like your face is a movie screen, showing me every step of your feelings."

"That's not true!" If it was, I was in deep doo-doo.

"It tells me enough."

"That much is probably true," I admitted, slapping my hand over my mouth way too late.

Sarah laughed. "At least you're perking up. That trick always works."

I shoved her shoulder with my hand. "Why do you always tell me when you're tricking me? If I even hint that I'm trying to, you get mad."

"Do you want to debate my hypocrisy or get naked?"

I started to say something, but then I had a flash. "You do it all of the time, don't you?"

"What?" She stepped closer to me. "Make love to you." Her breath was on my neck.

"You're cheating." Goose bumps spread over my body.

"Not seeing the problem from your viewpoint." She shoved me onto the bed, climbing on top.

I cupped her chin and said, "We'll discuss this issue later."

Her smile widened. "Looking forward to it."

"Not all of these talks will end up with sex, you know."

"You really have a limited imagination sometimes." Sarah's eyes glimmered with wanting, and she leaned down to kiss the hollow of my throat.

Together, we removed my top, and she nipped and licked her way to my right breast.

I let out a satisfied moan, knowing she was only getting started.

To prove my point, Sarah flicked my nipple with her tongue, making it hard, and she bit it gently at first, slowly adding more delightful pressure.

"I like this part of the discussion… a lot." I exhaled.

Sarah focused on the other nipple, taking her time.

It drove me mad with wanting, and even though I tried to stop them, my hips arched upward, pleading their case for attention.

Sarah looked up into my eyes, and I mouthed, "Please. Can't wait."

After one final flick of my left nipple, she began her trek down, kissing, nipping, and licking as her mouth and tongue descended.

Down and down she traveled, increasing my need.

It was like my clit hadn't been given proper attention in years, although it hadn't been that long ago. Who said lesbian bed death was a sure thing? They certainly never knew a couple like us.

Sarah was so close now.

"Oh God." I pressed my head into the pillow.

She reached the top of my jeans, kissing the sensitive skin.

Without being asked, I raised my buttocks for Sarah to strip off my jeans. My panties went next without much fanfare. It wasn't just me who wanted the whole tamale and fast.

Sarah's fingers softly raked my small patch of pubic hair. "I like that you stopped shaving it completely."

Her finger moved up and down my pussy lips, the wetness increasing. While she did this, Sarah kept a watchful eye on me, always curious how I reacted. Her delicate pink tongue wet her own lips like she was as turned on as I was.

I loved this moment. The one right before her mouth connected with my clit. I couldn't take my eyes off of her.

Sarah's head started to incline toward my pulsing.

My eyes grew large.

My lower body squirmed with anticipation.

Her mouth started to open.

I became even wetter.

Finally, even though it'd probably been a couple of seconds, her mouth made contact, and a tremor worked through my entire body.

Her finger still explored my folds. My hands fisted the sheets. One of her fingers separated my lips, and a tingling sensation zipped through me, starting at my midsection, bouncing to my toes, working its way up to my head, and then settling back where Sarah concentrated all of her efforts.

My hips rocked.

Sarah stayed centered with effort.

One of her hands slipped under my ass in an effort to keep me in place.

"Don't stop," I pleaded. "Please... don't... stop."

Her tongue circled my clit, and she added another finger, going in and out.

"Oh, Sarah." I writhed.

She dove in deep, causing my upper body to buck up. Sarah seemed to have anticipated this and moved in a way so not to break contact with her tongue.

I wanted to scream, which wasn't something I normally did. Was it because I knew I couldn't with a house full of people?

The orgasm started to crest, all of my nerve endings lighting up.

Sarah, with her knowledge of what I needed to tip over into bliss, thrust deep inside me, her tongue going into overdrive. My fingers dug into her skin.

The shudder started.

Another.

And, finally one more.

I fell back onto the bed, and Sarah stilled her fingers inside me, resting her chin on my pubic hair.

"It really is the best stress reliever," I said through ragged breaths.

She nodded.

I pulled her on top of me.

She swept hairs off my face. "Is this the time to ask you for a favor?"

"If you have to ruin the moment, sure."

A grin overtook her face. "Oh, nicely played."

"I learned from the best. Go ahead. Ask."

"Don't let this experience ruin you."

Totally confused, I asked, "Sex?"

"No. The pandemic. I see you slipping further and further from us. Studying more to keep your mind off of everything else. I need you to fight it, Lizzie. Please."

"Why is it okay to study the Gilded Age in an attempt to bond with Willow but not to study other things?"

"Some study is great. Trying to fill all of your free time with learning everything you can about every instant of human history is a sure way to lose your mind."

I had no idea how to confess the overwhelming need to still my mind, and the way for me to do that was by learning. Otherwise, darkness overtook me.

Sarah continued to drill her eyes into mine, so I said, "Fine," to put her mind at peace, knowing it wasn't a promise I could keep. She started to drift off to sleep, and my brain began to whir.

I was about to listen to an audiobook on JD Rockefeller, but it seemed wrong to go back on my promise so soon, so I cued up Hannah Gadsby's *Douglas* show on my phone. Surely, Sarah would approve of that.

While she slept, I watched the show with my headphones on.

CHAPTER NINETEEN

Friday, I tried to keep my shoulders back when I strolled into the kitchen for painting night.

"Okay, folks. I selected this one for my darling wife." Sarah batted her lashes at me, right in front of her mother. I tried not to vomit.

We all cued up the lessons on our laptops. The instructor was showing off what the end result should look like, and I zeroed in on the painted words: *Just Breathe*.

If Sarah was trying to be subtle in telling me I was the most uptight one of the bunch, she failed, but I painted on a smile and got to work, avoiding looking in her mother's direction.

The vase with flowers looked simple enough. Long brown streaks for the stems and tiny white blobs that looked more like deflated grapes than flowers, but whatevs. Given the simplicity, I was hoping we'd be done in an hour.

When sixty minutes had slowly passed, we were only halfway done.

How?

It was the easiest one we'd tackled, and it seemed to be taking forever.

During the break, Sarah moseyed over to see my canvas. "Wow, Lizzie. This is your best yet."

I tilted my head to the side. "It's o-kay," I stuttered, not wanting to jinx my mojo.

She placed a hand on my shoulder. "Honey, it's really good."

There was a lull in the conversation between all the couples, which turned out to be terrible timing because Rose ripped a massive fart. However, given her difficulties with her hearing, I was pretty sure she thought she'd gotten away with it. From the strained faces of Sarah, Maddie, Willow, and Troy, I wasn't the only one trying not to react.

It was mid-June, now, and the governor had let us out of lockdown. However, the virus wasn't under control, and everyone had opted to stay put, afraid another quarantine was on the horizon. Even I had to admit it was best to stay the course. And it killed me.

I met Sarah's eye, trying to quirk an eyebrow, but it only resulted with giving me eye strain.

After we finished our paintings, and again, I had to

admit mine wasn't half bad, I took my canvas to the office, my typical place to retreat at night.

Sarah slipped in with a glass of wine. "You going to hang it up?"

"Uh... I haven't decided."

"When it dries, you should."

I gave it the once-over again. "Yours is better. Maybe I should hang up yours."

"You can if you like, but I was going to hang mine up in our closet."

"That's an odd choice."

She hefted a shoulder and took a seat on the couch.

After leaning the painting against one of the bookcases, I joined her. "Are we going to talk about your mom?"

"In what way?"

"She's getting addled." I circled a finger around my temple.

"I'm hoping it's just a stage."

"She doesn't even know we can hear her farting. She's—" I realized I'd forgotten Rose's actual age, so I switched gears to "not eighty." I was fairly certain she was nowhere near her ninth decade.

"I know. Do you think it's the pandemic making her act so much older than she is?"

"I hope so. I know I have to set alarms for pretty much everything these days. Even when it's time to swap out my sweatpants." I added *study early onset dementia* to my ever-expanding list of things to delve into. After watching Hannah Gadsby, I had already started digging into autism, how it presented differently between boys and girls.

"This experience is pushing us all to the limits. Willow is certain she's going to lose her job. Enrollment at her school is plummeting for the fall. Also, they may try in-person teaching, and she doesn't feel comfortable doing that."

"I wouldn't either. So far, we're going remote." I let out a hiss of air. "Have you thought anymore about law school?"

Sarah sighed. "Part of me says do it because everyone is still here to help."

"The other?" I took a sip from my water glass.

"I'm so exhausted, and we're only trying to teach our kids the alphabet. Can you imagine if we had to homeschool elementary or middle school kids?"

"It's a relief we aren't. I'd hate for the children to get screwed out of actual learning. I fear how this will impact so many. They're like a lost school generation, and no one in power seems to know how to lead."

Sarah's silence meant she agreed, but from her closing her eyes, she was ready to call it a day.

## CHAPTER TWENTY

"Alright!" Maddie clapped her hands together. "I'm ready to watch about birders on a Saturday night. Nothing says exciting weekend plans like watching a show about people with binoculars. Is that a weird type of kink you're into Lizzie?" Maddie laughed, but she was alone.

"Oh, I've switched things around on the schedule, and I've decided we're going to watch *The Portrait of Wally* tonight." I clicked the TV on and navigated to the Amazon Prime home screen.

"I was just kidding." Maddie seemed genuinely apologetic.

"I know, and for the record, I changed my mind before the kink jab. Why do they make it so hard to search for a title?" I slowly clicked the arrow to start the tedious task of punching out each word of the title.

"I'm not in the mood for—" Maddie did her best

Nazi salute, which was disconcerting on many levels. She was pretty much spot-on, adding to my unease. She better not teach any of the children to do that while I was live on JJ's show.

"Too bad. I'm not prepared for the birder show." I finished tapping out *Portrait,* and the movie populated on the right-hand side of the screen, saving me from having to type out the rest in such a painstaking fashion.

"Why do you have to prepare?" Willow asked with obvious interest, moving to the edge of her seat. "Are you getting books for research? That sounds like fun."

"Uh, no." I panicked, trying to keep the news about my shirt to myself. "I meant… I need to be in the right head space, and I'm not."

"You have a tiny head like a bird. What else do you need to do to prep?" Maddie laughed at her own joke again, but this time Willow tugged on Maddie's arm as a way of saying *knock it off*.

Okay. I had to give her points for that.

Sarah, picking up on my annoyance as well, gave me a small smile.

"I'm ready to watch anything." Troy crammed white-cheddar cheese popcorn into his mouth, his favorite part of documentary night if his expanding belly was proof.

Rose rested her head on his shoulder. "Bring on Wally."

Sarah took the remote from me and started the

portrait documentary, putting the birder debate to rest. For the night at least. Maddie relished to continue pecking at me until getting me to crack like an egg.

Everyone watched in silence, and luckily for me, Maddie actually fell asleep.

When the credits started to roll, Willow got out her phone. "That was fascinating. I want to learn more."

"I have to admit it was much better than the other Nazi documentaries," Rose said in a way I think she meant to be encouraging, but I found it grating.

I understood not everyone enjoyed learning about them, but it was my specialty. However, maybe I shouldn't force my fascination with one of the evilest times in history on my housebound roommates. I'm the first to admit it wasn't everyone's cup of tea.

"I can't believe the museum fought giving it back to the family. If you ever find yourself siding with the Nazis, you're in the wrong." Sarah stretched her arms overhead, exposing a patch of skin, and my lady bits took note.

*Bad, Lizzie.*

Sarah's mom was in the room, and we were discussing the Nazis. Nothing should turn me on right now.

"There's a book about other pieces of art that were stolen." Willow displayed the screen on her phone, but I couldn't see it from across the room. "I'm going to get it. I must learn more!"

I nodded, trying not to show how much that irked

the shit out of me. Why hadn't I hopped onto Amazon right away to find this book? "I think I'm going to hit the hay."

"Would you like a copy of the book?" Willow asked.

"That's okay. Sarah said I can't take on anymore extracurricular studies." I whirled around. "Does that mean I shouldn't plan anymore documentary nights, because I still want to watch the birders one." I quickly added, "When the time is right."

"I never said you couldn't learn more." Sarah gave me the look that simultaneously screamed *don't throw me under the bus*, and *you misunderstood me*. "I wouldn't dream of taking your documentary privileges away, and you should study the topic with Willow."

Willow nodded, smiling, but there was a hint of mischievousness behind it. Had she sensed my excitement when I spied Sarah's stomach? Eww!

"Okeydokey," I said without much enthusiasm because I was trying to count how many days it'd been since I'd ordered my bird shirt, but my mind went blank.

When Sarah came into the bedroom, after one look at her face, I knew she wanted to slap me. Well, not physically, but she wasn't happy with me.

"She's really trying to be your friend, and your excuse for not taking part tonight was lame. Even for you." Sarah yanked her shirt over her head, but I was pretty certain she was simply getting ready for bed, not trying to turn me on, even if that was the outcome.

"I really hate it when you say even for me. Really, really, really hate it!" I tried fighting my turned-on state. This was becoming a trend for the pandemic. Sarah coming to bed upset with something I'd done, and while letting me have it, she also started stripping to get ready for bed, multitasking. It made my ability to think at all fly out the window.

"Don't try changing the subject." She shrugged into a sleep shirt.

"Why is it when I want to discuss something you do that upsets me, you claim it's not important?" My words flew out with way too much anger given it was also a statement I said about myself. I knew I was different.

"I'm sorry I used that phrase. I'll try not to do it in the future."

"Thank you. I'm not stupid." Knowing I was being a bit of a hypocrite didn't equate to me being able to downshift on my anger.

"Never said you were."

*You don't have to. I tell myself that all the time. Even more so lately.*

"Didn't you recently tell me not to keep hiding behind a book? I was only telling Willow I can't take on more."

"It's actually part of your subject area, and she bought a book about it. She was willing to learn about birds with you. You've always wanted to be a birder!" She dropped her jeans, and it was hard not to leer.

"I don't study art or birds," I defended weakly. "Besides, she didn't seem put off when I told her I'm not allowed. She's always smiling."

"It's her defense mechanism, Lizzie."

"Please. No one pays attention to me aside from you. She probably doesn't pick up half of the shit you do."

"You always say that, when in fact, people do pay attention to you. Just because your parents ignored you for so long, don't think everyone else does. I know for a fact that she looks up to you. A successful professor who makes regular appearances on JJ's show. You have so much going for you. But you're showing her it's better not to meet your heroes. Why can't you be nice and show an interest? It wouldn't kill you. It's fucking history. Your passion!"

"I'm no one's hero, and you don't know for sure this experience won't kill me."

"What does that mean?" Sarah crossed her arms over her chest.

"This situation is suffocating me. I never get alone time." I tugged at my collar before yanking my shirt off to slip on my Disney T-shirt, which had become my pajamas. "I've always needed my own space, but my office is now used by Willow, Troy, and even Rose when she wants to Zoom with her former cruising buddies."

"What do you call your closet time?" Sarah snapped.

I backpedaled. "You know about that?"

Sarah shook her head as if wondering how I could be such an idiot. "Of course, I know you hide out in the closet for an hour every morning."

"Did I leave my camp chair in there or something?" I'd been super careful, but I must have messed up somehow.

"You carry it up and down the stairs every single day. It's safe to assume everyone knows you're up to something."

"You see!" I jabbed a finger in the air. "That right there is part of the problem. Even when I'm trying to be sneaky, there are five pairs of eyes on the lookout."

"When you're trying to be sneaky?" She took her mom stance, including tapping her right foot.

"What? No. Don't get hung up on that. I used a poor choice of words. The point is—"

"I think you meant them," she cut me off.

"If you mean I want to be left alone, the answer is yes. I mean how would you have felt if I brought Unibrow home." Why did the man from the airplane pop into my head right then?

"Who's Unibrow?" Sarah's face screwed up in total confusion. "If you're referring to Willow, she doesn't have one."

"Correct. Nor does she have a widow's peak, which

I find odd given her name starts with a W and I. I don't get *that* at all!"

Sarah started to speak but stopped. Had she been going to say that was a stretch even for me and caught herself in time?

I rushed out, "That's not the point, though." I made frantic hand motions, trying to get my brain not to go down an idiotic path when we were discussing something important. It wasn't a simple ask because when my mind started racing, stopping it was the equivalent of putting the brakes on a freight train. Yeah, I'd get there, but not immediately.

"I have no idea what your point is." Sarah was doing her best not to lose her shit, probably because one of us needed to have a grip on reality, and it unfortunately fell upon her shoulders, making me feel oh-so-guilty.

"Don't do that!" I scolded.

"Do what?"

"Look for logic. All I'm trying to say is I didn't invite Unibrow to live with us. I could have, but I didn't because I don't like people." I dramatically cut the air with my hands.

"I still have no idea who Unibrow is, and why does this person need to move in?"

"He's no one, and he most definitely isn't moving in. I don't want to talk about Unibrow." I rued using this as a piece of evidence because it was wobbly at best and, more than likely, was quickly proving I was batshit crazy, a diagnosis I'd been battling for weeks now.

Sarah pressed her forehead into her palm. "You brought up Unibrow, and now you don't want to tell me who or what he is. You are talking about a person, aren't you? Can we at least establish that? Is it a student?"

"He's not important." I motioned for her to move on, but I added, "I mentioned it as proof I didn't invite people you don't know into our home without asking. I would never do that."

"First, you met Willow before she moved in, even if you don't remember." Sarah held up one finger, probably to mock mine still in the air, and then added another. "Two, if someone you know is in trouble, he can stay with us, and I wouldn't hold it against you. Three, I really think you need to calm down. You're getting worked up about things that are minor considering the big picture. Thousands of people are dying."

"How can I calm down when I can't even hole up in the closet without all of you knowing?" I was speaking in a loud, angry whisper. It was also possible I was acting like a jerk, but there was something inside me that wouldn't allow me to back down now that this particular genie was let out of the bottle. "I don't like having an interloper in my home."

Sarah stared at me, completely mystified, blinking excessively.

Maybe I lost her with the word *interloper*, so I

defined it for her. "It means someone who doesn't belong."

"I'm aware of the definition. I just can't believe how you're being such an asshole. Do I need to define that for you? How about I explain it this way? If you're not careful, you might spend all of your time alone, and you can study every aspect of human history. If you can't start being civil to Willow—"

"Are you threatening to kick me out of my own home during a pandemic over a woman with a ridiculous name?" Now, I was taking my jerkiness to a whole new level, and my heart, brain, and mouth were warring. My heart wanted me to stop arguing. My brain waffled to stand my ground and to stop hurting everyone's feelings, most especially the woman I loved more than anything. My mouth continued to spew out things without a care as to the meaning or consequences.

"Not during the pandemic, no. But it won't last forever."

"Are you sure? The world seems to be fucking up on a grand scale. We've been locked inside our home for so long, all the while millions of Americans are utterly convinced it's a hoax. It's simple science! I'm fucking tired of fuckwits with little to no common sense." I started to pace our bedroom.

She tried speaking, but I plowed on, "Then there's the whole issue of climate change. What will the world be like for our children when they grow up? I never thought I'd say this in earnestness, but when can we move to the moon?"

I continued my rant as I paced, "A cop leaned on a man's throat, killing him. Casey's black, meaning she can get shot at any moment, and odds are the shooter won't be held accountable and even less likely if a cop did it." I marched to the other side of the room. "JJ's daughter is Asian. Our asshole president is trying to pin his incompetence on China and keeps calling it the Chinese flu, upping hate crimes against Asians. Hate crimes across the board are through the roof." I took a deep breath. "I haven't even mentioned murder hornets. What happened to them? Are they still a threat?"

Sarah took a seat on the bed.

"Dad got Peter out of jail using every political connection he had, but what about everyone else in prisons who don't have a dad with money who can easily donate to Republicans and Democrats in exchange for favors. They're sitting ducks in there. It's not fair. I'm glad Peter's out, but I feel terrible for everyone else." I flipped around and made my way back to the other side of the room. "It's June, and infections seem to be slowing down, but mark my words, there's going to be a second wave in the fall that'll be worse than what we've already experienced. Thousands more are going to die. Alone and scared. I can't stand all of this nastiness in the world. It's driving me fucking insane, and all I want to do is cry all of the time!" I collapsed onto the bed, sobbing. "But I can't get a moment alone now that my closet secret is out," I said through ragged breaths.

Sarah wrapped me into her arms. "It's okay, Lizzie. It's going to be okay."

"It's not, though. This world is a terrible place, and I'm afraid for everyone I care about. I don't know if I have more room inside—" I grabbed the front of my shirt. "Because then I'll have to worry about them. Willow might not have a job in the fall. How do I solve that? I might not have one, but we're okay financially. Should I buy Maddie and Willow a house or condo? It can't be near us because I can't afford two mortgages in Wellesley, especially if I lose my university job. I'm not sure how most universities are going to survive this pandemic. Maddie won't want to be that far from Demi, so does that mean they have to live with us always? All these thoughts and worries—they're killing me! This is why I keep my head in a book. Otherwise, I can't stop the thoughts from swirling in my head." I jerked my upper body around like I'd been caught up in a tornado. "I'm so tired!"

"I need you to listen to me." She gripped my chin, forcing me to look her in the eyes. "Nothing is going to happen to anyone in our circle. Peter is safe. So are Casey and Mia. The Petries take care of those they love. All of us pitch in. It's not only on your shoulders. Yes, we don't know what will happen to Willow's job, but she's a grown-up, and she has Maddie, whose job is flourishing because everyone wants to redo their homes. I know you have a tendency to take everything on yourself, but don't. We'll get through this, and who knows? Maybe Casey will be the one to figure out how we move to the moon, and it'll be because you bought her a microscope and continued to pay for her Russian lessons."

I let out a combo of laughter and a snort. "How does a microscope and Russian equate to the moon?"

"You'll have to ask Casey that."

"You're just saying all this to calm me down."

"Is it working?" Her eyes were wide with alarm.

"A little, but Casey better hurry. Time is running—"

Sarah planted a wet kiss on my lips.

CHAPTER TWENTY-ONE

THREE DAYS AFTER OUR ARGUMENT ABOUT Willow, Sarah came into the office with two packages. One was a box, the other a floppy plastic bag.

"I thought we talked about this." Sarah held them up as if offering a sacrifice to the goddesses.

"Uh, can you refresh my memory?" I tapped the side of my head with a pen I'd been using to jot down notes from a book I was reading for my lecture scheduled on October nineteenth, which was months away, and I was still on summer break. I loved getting ahead of schedule, and the production calendar I'd constructed had made my academic life much easier to bite off in small chunks. Sadly, it was useless for my private life, and I took a stab in the dark. "You don't want to get the packages from the porch anymore?"

"Bad things happen when you order things online. If there are three of the same thing in these, I'm cutting you off." She was smiling, so I wasn't overly concerned.

More than likely, she was still testy about the Willow situation since I'd done nothing to address it. I didn't know how to say to her, "Hey, I'm an asshole for the first six months or so, but sometimes a switch will go off in my head and I'll deem you as okay. Slowly, if things work out, I'll start treating you decently, but don't rush me, or it's a deal breaker."

Wanting to keep things lighthearted between Sarah and me, I responded with an immature, "I have my own trust fund" and proceeded to stick my tongue out at her.

"Not the cutting off I meant."

"Oh, no naked time." I stiffened in my seat, balancing my pen between both index fingers. "That seems extreme considering I haven't really done anything wrong."

"None of these are yours?" She shook the box.

"I haven't ordered any books, and I have no idea what's in the plastic bag." An unease slid into the pit of my stomach, and I was sure I was forgetting something key.

"Both of them have your name on it." Sarah moved to the tables and knifed the seam of the box as if she was pretending it was my throat. Or so I imagined.

I stayed behind my desk, not out of fear, but I'd overdone it with the hand weights earlier, and my back was acting up.

After lifting the lid, Sarah whipped around, her eyes burning with satisfaction. "I knew it."

"What?" I had no idea what was in the box, and I hated feeling like I was missing the obvious, only proving I wasn't as smart as I thought.

Sarah held up a yellow hardcover book and read the title, "*Citizen Reporters: S.S. McClure, Ida Tarbell, and the Magazine That Rewrote America.*"

"Oh. I used one of my credits for the audiobook, but I don't remember requesting the hardcover." Again, I scratched my head with my pen.

"Maybe you clicked two buttons?" Luckily for me, she didn't sound so convinced, but the anxiety continued to churn in my stomach, and my extremities turned ice-cold.

"I have no idea." I searched for the order online. "All I can see is the audiobook. Did *they* mess up? The pandemic is fraying everyone's nerves."

Sarah stood behind me, still wearing the gardening gloves. "That's weird. Why couldn't it accidentally send a box of truffles."

"That would be better. Please don't be mad at me. I didn't order the book."

"Honey, I'm not mad. I know you struggle with ordering things, but I'm not angry. It's kind of cute, the way simple things mess you up, and I don't think it reflects on your intelligence, so please wipe the fear off your face." She placed her garden-gloved hands on my shoulder, but that only made me squirm, because I hated being near dirt.

As if she guessed the reason for my unease kicking up a notch, Sarah stripped her gloves off and dropped them onto the floor.

"Maddie's used the account before for household things. Maybe she got it for Willow as a gift. Is it her birthday?"

"Not that I know of, and if she did, it would be in our orders."

"Right." I scanned the orders again, going back weeks to make sure. "I don't see it, but it won't go to waste. I'm enjoying the audiobook. I'm sure I'll underline some passages so it doesn't feel left out." I hated for my research books not to feel loved and appreciated.

"What else is in the box?" Sarah wasn't asking me but the Amazon gods or something. Leaning over, she replaced her gloves and went back to the box.

Maddie popped her head into the library. "Hey, did a package come? Willow's expecting some books. She shipped them in Lizzie's name to be safe because she accidentally sent some items to her apartment."

"Aha!" I sat up straighter, ruing doing so when a spasm worked through my lower back. "Ouch."

Neither Sarah nor Maddie noticed.

"Yeah, it's here." Sarah took the remaining books out of the box. "*A Dirty Year: Sex, Suffrage, and Scandal in*

*Gilded Age New York* and *The Meaning of Mariah Carey*." Sarah gave Maddie a puzzled look.

"The last one is for me. Being around historians is making me want to learn things."

I was able to curb the impulse to say reading trash about Mariah Carey didn't count, because Sarah had lectured me in the past about being a snob. Reading was good, no matter the subject.

Maddie took the books and left the room.

"What mystery item is in the plastic bag?" Sarah held it in the air as if unsure about opening it.

"Only one way to find out." I acted out cutting it open with scissors.

Sarah started to speak but ripped the plastic bag open. "What in the fuck is this?"

She held up my T-shirt that read *Nice Tits!*

"It came." I gingerly got out of my chair, walked over to her, and held it up to me. "I've decided to take my birding interest to the next level."

"This is the best news I've had today."

Letting my hands fall, I asked, "Why?"

"Because those are the only tits you're going to have access to for a very long time," she said in all seriousness.

I gaped at her. "Why are you being a mean lady? You said you'd cut me off if there were three in the bag. There's only one. Right?" I craned my neck to see if it was empty.

"Desperate for more tits?"

"Isn't everyone?"

Her sternness melted away, and she started to laugh.

"So, earlier, that was a joke?"

She nodded.

"Phew, because I'd rather have real tits to play with. I mean your boobs, not actual birds." I shook about as if I'd walked through a cobweb. "How can they be so cute but scary?"

She continued laughing.

"Hey. Can you keep this quiet? I wanted to wear it when we watch the birding documentary."

"Aha! That was what you meant when you said you weren't prepared. What a relief. I really thought part of your closet time was dedicated to learning everything about birds. I feared you would ultimately decide you needed field research and head to a jungle, where we would lose you forever."

"Don't be silly. I could never survive living in a jungle."

"I know, hence the losing you part." She placed a hand on my cheek. "You can be adorable sometimes."

"Is that because I have nice tits?" I held up the shirt again.

"And a nut. You're a nut."

"I've been called worse things." I kissed her cheek. "Mum's the word about my shirt, okay?"

## CHAPTER TWENTY-TWO

I sat in my office chair, holding my shirt against me, wishing I could put it on, when Maddie crashed into the door.

"What in the world?" Her eyes boggled, and I worried they'd pop out of her head.

"Don't you knock?" I dropped the shirt into my lap, but the damage had been done.

"Does that say *Nice Tits*?" She burst into laughter. "Are you trying to wean yourself off your grapefruit fetish?"

"I don't have a thing for grapefruits!" I growled.

"Are you sure? Because I've been watching you massage a massive double D size one every morning, and I can tell you're thoroughly enjoying it."

"It seems to be the only part of my life I can control right now." I circled a hand in the air.

"Whoa." Maddie sat on one of the chairs opposite mine. "Talk to me."

"I am. I categorically don't want to fuck a grapefruit. No ambitions on that front at all."

"That's not what I mean. Why are you so...?" She acted out uptight.

"I hurt my back this morning lifting weights."

She studied me. "I think it's more than that."

"I'm fine. Really."

"Is it the pandemic? Having everyone here? Are you worried about your job?"

Phew!

She hadn't guessed my autism fear. Ever since listening to a few books on the subject, I couldn't help noticing that I ticked a lot of the boxes. Like all of them. Why did I have to watch that Hannah Gadsby clip? Why had Ethan sent it to me? Had he thought *It's time Lizzie faces some hard truths?*

To Maddie, I said, "Ding, ding, ding," and made a chiming noise to drill it home those were my only worries.

"Everything's going to be okay. The pandemic can't keep going—"

"It's not like we're really trying as a whole to squash it. They're opening the country back up when every single person should be in lockdown. Not just here but the world. I understand the economic devastation is terrible, but it's only going to get worse and prolonged the longer the illness lasts."

"I agree, but the problem with having seven billion individuals is not everyone has common sense. The majority of people don't."

I leaned back into my seat. "I guess my bird shirt won't be a surprise now."

"I'm not following. How is that connected to COVID?"

"It isn't. I bought this"—I hoisted it off my lap—"to wear on the night we're going to watch the birders documentary. I thought it'd be funny."

"Oh! Your secret is safe with me."

"Yeah, right," I scoffed, dropping the shirt into my lap again.

"Hey now!" At least she had the decency to wear a sheepish smile, despite her asking, "What are you insinuating?"

"You love busting my chops and pointing out all of my oddities for the group to laugh at."

"Okay, I know I do that on occasion—"

"Does that word mean *all the time* in your head?"

"Don't press my buttons. I'm trying to help you."

I eyed her with suspicion. "What's the catch?"

She grinned, knowing I wasn't that stupid. "If you start actually taking part in the history club with Willow, I'll—" She mimed zipping her lips shut. "She's been buying Nazi books in hopes of finding a way to talk to you. Apparently, she's intimidated by you."

"Me?" I placed a hand on my chest.

"I guess you have a reputation in the academic

scene as being esteemed or something." Maddie said the words in a way for me to know she knew it was true, but she couldn't stop herself from teasing me. I wondered what personality defect she had.

"I don't—" I shifted in my chair. "I just try harder than most."

Maddie regarded me. "Why do you do that?"

"What?"

"Talk bad about yourself when you know you do have a sterling reputation?"

"Habit, I guess."

"Stop it. Only I can knock you down a peg or two." She seemed to be deadly serious about this statement.

"You do excel at it."

"Everyone has to have a hobby. You have tits and grapefruit. I have sarcasm."

"For the last time, I don't have a thing for grapefruits!"

"Just tits?" She winked at me. "When can I tell Willow about your first official meeting?"

"Soonish."

"I'm going to hold you to it, and you need to talk to your brother. He misses you." With that directive, Maddie left the room.

CHAPTER TWENTY-THREE

The following day, when I entered the kitchen, Sarah barked, "Have you talked to Peter yet?" She used an apple corer, pressing down, until making contact with the cutting board.

I swiped one of the slices. "Nope."

"Stop that. It's going to be tart." She took it back.

"I love a good tart." I waggled my brows. "You aren't feeding them to the kids, are you?"

"I'm baking a pie."

"You are?" Sarah hadn't been the baking type before the pandemic.

She opted not to explain the pie and asked, "Why not? I'm sure he'd love to hear from you."

*Yes, but what about Demi?*

Luckily, Olivia, with her tennis racquet, wandered into the kitchen, eager for her lesson, which involved the two of us messing about on the grass in the backyard because we didn't want her taking lessons with other kids right now.

I hunched down. "Is it time for smash ball?"

She nodded with such eagerness and slammed her racquet against the floor, I shot Sarah a worrisome look, but she simply shrugged it off.

I took Olivia's hand and said to Sarah, "Gotta run to bond with Olivia, right, baby girl?"

Ollie nodded.

Sarah smiled, but her eyes said we weren't done with the Peter conversation, and I wondered if Maddie had been nagging Sarah about it.

In the backyard was a covered bucket with a lot of tennis balls. Given Ollie was so young, our lessons involved me bouncing the ball on the parched lawn and her chasing it down with her racket to whack it, usually striking after the third or fourth bounce, making it look more like golf. But it was our daily activity for the two of us, and we didn't care how we looked.

"Are you ready, Ollie?" I held a tennis ball in the air.

"Sm-mash!" She held the racket in a menacing fashion, which I think was the real reason she loved this sport. Olivia, as Sarah liked to say, was the Petrie Enforcer.

It was only slightly intimidating, and from what I read, not all that worrisome given her age. Not yet, at least.

I tossed another ball, watching her scramble and take errant swipes at it, giggling the whole time.

"You're so good at this game," I encouraged.

I wasn't a sports person, so I had no idea if she had any real talent. To me, it was about her having fun and getting outdoor time. If this infernal plague ever subsided, and she wanted to continue playing, I'd get her enrolled in lessons.

"Okay. We have to collect all the balls!" I used my silly voice and clapped my hands like the task was the most exciting thing in the world, not simply a way to keep track of the balls because it was becoming more difficult to get certain items delivered to the house.

Ollie scampered about, gathering them and putting them back into the bucket. "Again, Mommy."

"You got it!"

After this round, she lost interest in the hunting and gathering stage, so when Maddie called her in for a snack, I stayed outside to hide all the balls from the pesky neighborhood dog I was convinced had his eye on them. That was the only explanation for why one of them had been left in a mangled mess in a pile of drool.

Someone let Gandhi out, so I stayed in the sunshine a bit longer, keeping an eye on him. Sure enough, he dropped a load, and I shoveled it into the trash. It seemed with kids and pets, I spent the majority of my time picking up shit. Literally.

When I got back inside, Maddie handed me her phone. "Peter wants to say hi."

I glanced down at the screen, seeing my bearded brother. "Hey there."

Maddie and Sarah waved their arms that I should take the phone into a different room to have a heart-to-heart with my older brother.

I withheld a sigh but did as directed.

Settling into a chair in my office, I asked, "How are you?"

He sneezed.

I shot to high alert instantly. "You don't have COVID, do you?"

He sniffled. "No. Just allergies."

"Are you sure? Have you been tested?"

Peter gave me his confident smile. "I'm positive."

"That answer doesn't mean you've been tested."

"How's Demi?"

I shouldn't have been surprised he changed the subject, since I would have done the same if I was in his shoes, not wanting to discuss something I'd rather forget. "She's turning into quite the artist. It's funny. All of the kids have their own specialty. Fred and his drums. Ollie and tennis. Demi and art."

"What about Calvin?"

"So far, he's a pro at napping and cuddling."

"Everyone has to start somewhere." He offered a kind smile, but his eyes were troubled.

Was the root cause the same as mine?

"What's your plan now?" I carefully lifted the lid on the potential can of worms involving Demi. Before heading to prison, he'd given up parental rights, thinking he'd be inside for years.

"Nothing, really. I can't leave the house. Well, I guess it's not advisable for anyone right now, but I have an electronic device on my ankle to ensure I don't." He aimed the camera on the phone so I could see it.

"I'm sorry, Peter."

"Not your fault. I'm lucky I got out." He sneezed again.

How could I ask now that he wasn't incarcerated if he wanted me to bring Demi to him? Legally, Sarah and I were her parents now, but did he want to reassume his rights over her? Was that even possible?

"How are you getting along with Willow?" he asked.

Blown away he knew about Willow, I didn't know what to say, so I hefted a helpless shoulder.

"Yeah." He chuckled. "That pretty much sums up what I heard."

I sat up straight in my desk chair. "What do you mean?"

"Maddie says you haven't taken a shine to her."

I rested my chin on my free hand. "It's kinda weird."

"Maddie really likes her, and she deserves happiness."

This was odd coming from Peter since I was 98.675 percent convinced he was still madly in love with Maddie. Although, he had been the one who encouraged me to take Maddie with me when I moved from Colorado so she could live her life.

"I know," I conceded.

"I read Willow's book on the Gilded Age. Man, it sure sounds a lot like how things are now. The rich get insanely richer, and the rest are simply fucked."

I chuckled, because our family was in the richer category, and he could thank his semi-free status on our dad's money and influence. "Kettle. Pot. Black."

He offered a hangdog smile. "Yep. Still, though, I'd like to see things change. For *your* kids' sakes because what we have now isn't sustainable for decades to come."

The way he stressed *your* put my mind at ease, and it was done in such a Petrie way. To speak in code because we avoided icky things like feelings. Our mom drilled into our heads they were for the weak. It was best to power through everything and not address anything that would cause fear. Keep your head down, and keep going.

"Have you read her book?" Peter pulled me out of my thoughts.

I shook my head.

"Read it, Lizzie. Please."

Again, that was Petrie code to say, "Give Willow a chance."

"Okay."

"Not good enough. Promise me." He gave me his best big brother glare, which still took getting used to because he hadn't been a great sibling for the majority of my life.

It actually worked on me, though, and I said, "I promise."

We ended the call, and there was a knock on the office door. "Come in, Maddie."

"It's me, actually." Willow stood in the doorway.

"Oh. Did Maddie send you in for her phone?" I showed her the device and waved her in.

"I can take it to her, but you got a package." Using a tissue, Willow clutched a plastic bag by its corner.

"Thanks."

She set it on the table, looking at me as if she expected something else.

Had Peter gotten a message through to Maddie via Sarah's phone that I had promised to give Willow a chance?

"Should I open it? I know you hate germs." Willow put on the garden gloves sitting on the table.

"That'd be nice. Thank you."

Maybe she wasn't all that bad.

That thought flew out of my head when Willow started snickering.

"What's up?" My shoulders tensed.

She removed her gloves and grasped a red shirt in each hand for me to see.

"Oh, no. I got three *Nice Tits!* shirts?" Sarah had said she'd cut me off if I had another ordering mishap. I was pretty sure she didn't mean it, but did I really want to take that chance?

Willow looked to one hand and then the other.

"One came just the other day." I tapped my fingertips against the desk.

"They're hilarious."

"They're becoming a problem."

"Why?" She took a seat. "You can never have too many tits."

"I suck when it comes to placing orders or doing simple things." I slumped in my seat, my autism secret weighing heavily on me.

"From my viewpoint, it worked out to your favor. Less laundry in between wearing one of the funniest shirts. Hands down." She continued chuckling but stopped suddenly. "I know. You should wear this when we watch the birding documentary. Is that tonight?"

How had she figured out my plan? I'd casually mentioned the doc was lined up for today now that the shirt had finally arrived.

"That was my plan, but Sarah and Maddie have already seen the other one and now you. It won't be much of a surprise." I slid further down into my chair.

"They've only seen one. Not three."

"I rather Sarah didn't find out about—" I motioned to the two on her lap and sighed. "She's going to find out, isn't she?"

"I've got an idea." Willow looked over each shoulder to ensure we were alone.

* * *

"Okay, team, we're going to wander in there like nothing is going on." Willow looked to me and then Troy.

Troy held out the hem of his shirt, which was a little snug, laughing.

Willow nudged his shoulder. "Stop," she said, doing her best not to laugh.

It was hard for me to control my own giggling.

After we each took a deep breath, we wandered into the family room for documentary night.

"Oh. My. God." Maddie's mouth gaped open. "We're surrounded by titties."

"What are you three wearing?" Rose squinted.

"What? Nothing." Willow took the lead, settling next to Maddie as if none of us was wearing a shirt reading *Nice Tits!*

Following her example, I sat next to Sarah, and Troy took position near Rose. When Sarah had mentioned getting such a large sectional when we moved, I had no idea we'd actually put it to use, but here we all sat, comfortably.

"Pass me the popcorn," Troy said, holding his hand out to Willow.

"Sure thing." Willow happily handed it off.

"I knew it," Sarah whispered in my ear.

"What?" I prepared for her to mention my ordering mishap because it was right in front of her.

"You and Willow would get along eventually." Sarah snuggled against my arm. "Let's learn about birding in Central Park."

I started the video.

After a few minutes, I met Willow's eye and mouthed, "Thank you."

Troy handed me the popcorn bowl, and I shoved some into my mouth, but then something on the screen caught my attention. I tried to speak but nearly choked.

Sarah paused the TV. "You okay?"

"It's him!" I pointed at the man on the screen, while drinking water to clear my throat.

"Who?" Sarah asked.

"Chris Cooper."

"Who's that?" Maddie asked. "He looks familiar."

"He's the black guy that white woman tried calling the cops on, claiming he attacked her in the park. Remember. She lost her job."

Recognition flashed across everyone's face.

"It is him," Willow said.

"I remember reading that he likes to go birding in Central Park." I studied his kind eyes. "It makes you sick, doesn't it? That someone tried getting him arrested for no reason. Why can't we all just get along?"

Sarah wrapped an arm around me. "It would be nice."

After letting out a frustrated sigh, I restarted the video, not able to shake the feeling that hatred would never be eradicated. My eyes wandered over everyone on the sectional, and I started to wonder if there was hope considering it took Sarah time to accept Troy, and I needed to get used to Willow. Would the pandemic bring others together or tear them apart?

CHAPTER TWENTY-FOUR

On Sunday morning, it was roughly half past eight, and the kids were fed and in the playroom with Rose and Troy. In the kitchen, I grabbed a grapefruit from the bottom drawer of the fridge. Was it a double D, like Maddie had claimed the other day? Not that I had much experience with boobs of that size. It wasn't like I could compare the fruit to my own tiny tits, so I did the next best thing and held it level with my head, to look at the reflection in the window. It was nearly the same size.

Had I never noticed how massive they were until I started hand-washing them? Actually, even then I hadn't noticed. Maddie did. Were they larger this year because orchards were short of pickers, resulting in a longer growing window? Was the 2020 batch mutant grapefruit, fitting the theme for the year?

Whatever the case, I turned on the hot water and stood at the sink, lost in thought, while scrubbing.

"I know you've denied having a citrus fetish, but maybe you should check out your face when you wash one." Maddie poured a cup of coffee. "According to the experts, they've figured out you can't catch the plague from surfaces."

"It's part of my routine now." I shrugged, cleansing it for another ten seconds before I took a fresh towel from a drawer to dry it.

"You just like boob-shaped objects." She laughed at her own joke.

"Correct me if I'm wrong." I set the grapefruit on my plate. "You have a girlfriend now."

"Yes." Maddie scrunched her nose, not following my train of thought.

"One that you like." I sliced the fruit in half, placing one section into a container for tomorrow morning.

She nodded. "A lot."

"Then why are you still picking on me? You should be picking on her." I pointed the knife at her before placing it next to the sink. Sarah insisted they be hand-washed and not placed in the dishwasher.

"I think you missed the part about me liking her a lot." Maddie leaned against the counter.

I stared at her. "Exactly. If you don't show her your true personality now, you're just lying. I've noticed during the past few months, you only give me this much shit when she isn't around. Sometimes, when you slip with her present, she encourages you to stop. Maybe you should think about that."

"That's not..." Worry clouded her eyes. Maddie finished with, "true," but the denial had flamed out of her tone.

I selected a spoon from the cutlery drawer and carried my breakfast to my office, bumping into Sarah.

"Whoa! Where's the fire?" She steadied the coffee mug, ensuring it didn't slosh over the side.

"Have you checked the kitchen?" I asked, sniffing. "My allergies are acting up, and I'm pretty stuffy." I tried detecting smoke again but couldn't smell a thing even if a fire was right below my nose. "This state is making my allergies worse than normal. I should see a doctor when things get back to normal. If they do."

"I was asking why you're storming into your office."

"What...? Oh. I'm running late this morning, and Maddie was being her usual charming self. She has it in her head I have a thing for grapefruit."

Sarah studied my face. "I'll talk to her about letting up. Sometimes, I don't think she knows how to tease you in an acceptable way."

"I don't want the kids to learn from her. There's good-natured ribbing, and then there's Maddie. The more she does it, the more I'm getting fed up with it." And, the other night, I had started to think we could all survive together.

"I can see that."

I let out an angry breath. "Just because I'm different doesn't give her the right to treat me poorly."

"I absolutely agree."

"I should get to work. I need to gather my sources for my twenty-second lecture for next semester. I love getting ahead of schedule." I lifted half of my English muffin and chomped into it, making sure the crumbs went onto the plate.

"Can you spare a minute? I have an idea you might like." Her eyes glowed in the way when she was about to propose something I should like, but she still used her cautious tone, meaning in all probability I wouldn't take to the proposal right off the bat.

Not that I relished going Red Lizzie, but it was a part of me. A big part of me and growing even more since the start of the pandemic.

I didn't say anything but stared into her eyes, waiting for the blow.

"Let's go into your office." Sarah prodded me with a bump of her hip.

"I have a Zoom call in forty-five minutes, and I want to eat breakfast first."

"You can eat while I talk." She guided me through the door.

"I see how this is going to be." I sat at my desk since it was nearly impossible to eat grapefruit while sitting on a couch without getting all sticky, and I hated when my hands got dirty.

Sarah settled into one of the wingbacks, taking a deep breath. "I think we need time to ourselves."

I cranked my neck upward with such a ferocity I'm surprised my head didn't snap off completely. "Are you finally asking everyone to move out?"

Sarah's grin didn't fall, and I suspected she was forcing it to stay in place. "Even better."

"We're moving?" I wasn't particularly fond of the prospect, but if it gave me the space I was in such a desperate need for, why not?

Her forced smile started to falter, but she persevered. "Not that either. We're going away for your birthday weekend. Just you and me."

"July fourteenth is on a Tuesday this year."

"I know. We're going the weekend before."

I closed one eye, my habit when confused, as if I would be able to see the answer better. I knew it didn't make sense, but I couldn't stop myself from doing it. "I don't know if you've heard of this little thing called COVID-19?"

"Nope. Haven't heard of it. Do share."

I didn't like her tone. "Seriously. The numbers are spiking in Europe because of travelers going abroad, mostly to Spain. Travel is a bad idea. Terrible."

"Good thing we're not going to Europe and most especially not Spain."

"We most definitely aren't going to Maine because we can't, and if we go to Vermont, we have to quarantine for fourteen days, making it difficult to get away for one weekend." My mind raced, trying to remember all of the travel details for every surrounding state. "If you think I'm getting on a plane, you've lost your damn mind."

"We're going to the Berkshires."

"Why? The only thing I know about them is that's where rich people go. Or did."

"Because we need time together. Alone."

"But—"

"We're staying in a historic inn that has a restaurant with outside seating. One word: bacon. You love having bacon on trips." Her eyes glowed with victory.

Damn her.

She'd tossed in historic and bacon on purpose to tame my instinct to flat out refuse.

"I'm listening," I said with hesitation in my voice.

"We'll drive there, so no chance of infection on the way. I've made reservations to visit the Norman Rockwell museum. They have limits per room, and everyone has to wear a mask. We have dinner reservations at Naumkeag—"

"At what?"

"It's a Gilded Age mansion, and we're having a picnic on the grounds at sunset."

"As in outside?"

"That is the definition of picnic." She playfully raised her eyebrows. "The next day, we have a reservation to visit The Mount, Edith Wharton's home. Again, they have limits on the people allowed inside and masks are a must, even when wandering the garden."

I slowly chewed a bite of grapefruit as Sarah sipped her coffee, her smugness radiating off of her.

Finally, I said, "Well played."

Sarah pressed her palms together. "I knew you couldn't resist. Thank God you've been studying the Gilded Age and reading Wharton's books, or your stubbornness might have prevailed. I really need to get away. Which part sealed the deal for you? The historic inn or bacon?" She took another sip of coffee.

"Neither."

She quirked her eyebrow, waiting.

"Time away from everyone—er, alone time with you."

She laughed. "It was the Gilded Age aspect, wasn't it?"

"Not going to say." I avoided her eyes.

Sarah squealed. "I knew it. You, my dear, are easy to play."

"So are you." I blew a kiss at her. "I have to hop on my call."

At three, Fred came in squawking, "Walk, Mommy!"

"I never have to set an alarm for Freddie time." I snapped my laptop shut. "Let's get ready."

It was a stunning July day, and we both wore shorts and T-shirts.

Freddie chirped at a bird in a tree.

The bells of the church around the corner started to chime, and I glanced at my watch, knowing it wasn't noon, but why were the bells tolling now? I had to get used to hearing them every day.

"Bells," Freddie said.

"Yep. It must be a special day or something." Being an atheist, I didn't get religion.

We rounded a corner and nearly ran smack dab into a bunch of people wearing black. I gripped Freddie's hand, pulling him and Gandhi back. While my eyes adjusted, I saw all of them. Nuns in their full garb heading right for us.

"Je-hoshaphat f-fudging Christ-mas!" While I cringed over stuttering every word, I was greatly relieved I avoided saying *Jesus fucking Christ*. Not simply because I had Freddie with me, but this was not the right crowd for such an offensive blasphemy.

One of the nuns looked over her shoulder and laughed.

Fred started to chant *Christmas*, causing more of the strangers to smile.

My mind couldn't comprehend what we'd run into.

Soon, more people passed by us, including serious looking men in church robes. Some of them carried candles, and one had a cross. It was the strangest thing to witness outside of a church, and I wasn't a church-goer, so I'd never seen it aside from in movies.

Fred seemed taken by the religious parade, and we watched them continue along their way. Even if we wanted to, it'd be hard to get past them without diving into the crowd, and I didn't think that was the right course.

When we got home, Sarah greeted us at the door.

Fred said, "Fudging Christmas!"

"That's a new one." Sarah kissed the top of his head, and he headed for the kitchen for his snack. "Anything I should know about?"

"I'm pretty sure the world is ending." I hung Gandhi's leash up in the entryway closet.

"Nothing new, then."

"2020 keeps on giving."

"Speaking of that…" Sarah pulled me into the office. "Willow lost her job."

"Who fires someone on a Sunday?" My mind drifted back to the nuns. Had they been an evil omen or something?

"I think it happened on Friday, but Maddie just told me."

"What's Willow going to do?"

## CHAPTER TWENTY-FIVE

"There's the inn!" Sarah squealed from the passenger seat, tapping her feet on the car floor. "I can't believe we're having a weekend away. I so need this."

I ducked down, scanning the street and entrance of the hotel. "Where do I park?"

"Turn at the corner. There should be spots in the back."

I did as she said and drove slowly down the side street, only seeing dead ends behind shops probably for delivery trucks. Finally, there was a gravel parking lot, and I pulled in. It was divided into different quarters, but it all seemed to be for the inn, given the signage.

"This place seems much bigger than I expected," I said, not liking the truth. Did that mean there would be a lot more people than I was prepared for?

"It's going to be fine. Everyone has to wear a mask." Sarah gave my thigh a squeeze.

I killed the engine. "Let's check in."

We entered a door that read *Entrance*, but it led to a series of hallways, and there were zero clues for how to navigate to the front desk, which seemed odd considering how many signs they had in the parking lot.

Sarah, standing about ten feet away, asked someone on the housekeeping crew for directions, but instead of telling us, she motioned with a hand we should follow her. The route involved so many twists and turns I was starting to get dizzy.

I whispered in Sarah's ear, "I should never leave the room without adult supervision."

Not laughing, she nodded in complete agreement. "I might never see you again."

There were two guests at the front desk, each separated by more than six feet, and there was plexiglass between the guest and hotel employee. We stood on the taped spot on the rug in their effort to enforce the six feet rule. The lobby was cavernous and dark. Adding to the eerie feel, the lights were off, which wasn't so bad since it was three in the afternoon. I wondered if they kept the lights off to hide the oldness of the building. Given it was a historical inn, I wasn't surprised to see the lobby filled with antique sofas and chairs. But there was a fine line between quaint antiques and simply ancient and in disrepair.

Sarah raised an eyebrow at me, but neither of us commented on the shabbiness of the place.

After waiting for over five minutes, Sarah retreated to one of the sofas, taking a seat, while I stayed in line.

For another five long minutes.

It seemed both individuals at the front desk had serious issues that needed addressing, given the redness of their faces. As my eyes continued to wander the worn carpet and dust on all the knickknacks on the shelves and above every doorframe, my gut told me this wouldn't be the most pleasant place to sleep. Still, we were away from the house, and aside from my face getting particularly moist from the mask, I was determined not to let my inner grouch out. Sarah had gone to a lot of trouble to arrange everything.

An angry and dissatisfied woman cleared out, and the hotel staff member took a deep breath before waving me forward.

I supplied our last name and waited for the woman to pull up our reservation in the computer. Soon enough, I was filling out a health certificate, stating I didn't have a fever or any symptoms. I ticked all the appropriate boxes and added my signature, sliding the paper under the plexiglass.

Through the opening, the woman handed me two keys. Old fashioned ones. They were taking the historical element to heart.

"Is this on the fourth floor?" I asked, looking at the room number.

"Yes. There's a staircase right around the corner, or down the hallway to the left is the elevator."

I nodded and said thanks.

Sarah's eyes were scanning the décor, which heavily favored teapots and the types of fancy plates meant to be hung on a wall, not used for meals.

"Do you think we can get a cup of tea here?" I joked.

Sarah's face hardened, and I kicked myself for cracking the joke.

*Remember, Lizzie. She went to a lot of effort.*

"Elevator or stairs?" I held up the keys. "We're on the fourth floor."

"Elevator."

I grabbed the handle of our rolling bag and waved for Sarah to walk ahead of me.

"Such a charmer." She batted her lashes over her shoulder.

"What can I say? I'm into views."

"Wh—?" My meaning hit her. Shaking her head, she said, "This might be a long weekend." From her tone and extra twist of her hips, though, I was certain my comment had the impact I wanted.

We made it down one hallway and took a right down another.

"The lady said it wasn't far." I adjusted my mask since it'd slipped down my nose.

"I think she lied."

"Do you feel like we're in a horror film? None of

the hallways are labeled, and the paths seem to go against common sense."

Sarah stopped to check out an old Hollywood poster. "The decorations are interesting. Maybe the original owner had a thing for teapots, and one of the grandkids loves classic movies."

"Or they bought everything at garage sales. Maybe they'll have one of those beds where you can insert a quarter to make it shake."

"Ah—" Sarah pointed down a different hallway with a sign for the elevator. "Follow me, dear."

"Gladly."

Again, Sarah glanced over her shoulder, this time giving me shade. Was it me not so discreetly checking out her ass or the crack about the hotel bed?

"Don't distract me. I want to see your curves." I waved for her to keep walking.

She rolled her eyes but put more oomph into her hip twist. "You're lucky we're here to celebrate your birthday."

"Hard to believe we have four kids. You're a fucking knockout."

"Such the sweet talker today. But don't think a compliment will get you off the hook for fetching me coffee in the morning."

"That's what came to your mind? And, I'm the strange one." I stopped in front of some children's drawings. The type you'd see in the hallways of an elementary school, not a hotel. "This is a weird place."

"The drawings are adorable, though." She rested her masked face on my shoulder.

"They are, but when you put them next to that chest of drawers"—I pointed at the piece of furniture listing to the left—"which is almost the same as the ten others we've meandered by on this long walk to our room, it's odd. Nothing in this place makes sense. And, how old is this carpet?" I stared down at my feet, expecting to see swirls of dust.

"It's seen better days."

We stumbled upon a staircase.

"Let's walk up," Sarah said. "I'm not sure I trust the elevator here anyway."

We did, and when we reached our floor, we had to go left, then right, according to the numbers and arrows on plaques.

Sarah scanned the numbers on the doors and said, "We're two down."

At the door, I fished the key from my pocket. "Fingers crossed it's not a nightmare." I swung the door open, and my eyes spied the bed. "Shit."

Sarah carefully stepped into the room, still reserving judgment.

"Ten bucks the mattress is made of straw."

She eyed it dubiously. "It's possible. The wallpaper is interesting."

"Is that your way of saying hideous?"

"It's like they redid the room in the eighties and haven't done a lick of work since." Her eyes followed the seams where the paper was peeling away from the walls, and one section had a square of an entirely different type of wallpaper. While the colors matched, the size of the flowers didn't.

"I don't think they've cleaned the place since the eighties, either." I shook a finger at a hole in the bedspread and then at a black, tarlike smudge near the pillow, making me wonder how badly stained it was at the foot of the bed since it was tucked into the space between the mattress and footboard, out of sight. "I really hope we aren't paying much for this torture."

"We got a hundred dollars off."

"A hundred? How much do they charge for this place?" I placed the bag on a metal luggage rack by the wood desk.

"Three hundred and fifty a night."

"Wait. Are you telling me we're paying two hundred and fifty dollars to stay in a rundown shithole simply because they put historic in the name?" My eyes saw something weird by the window. "What's that?"

Sarah marched to the rope and read the sign dangling from the wall. "Apparently this is an old rope ladder for climbing out the window in case of a fire." She added, "But it says not to use it now. It's only here for the historical aspect."

"I wonder how many people have wanted to hang themselves with it after staying here for a night."

Sarah gave the room another once-over. "Let's set our things down and not return until bedtime."

"So we don't have to see anything?"

"Exactly!"

"Are you getting the feeling that 2020 is simply a test of endurance to see who can survive?"

"Ah, there's my positive wife." She kissed me on the lips. "Get me out of here."

CHAPTER TWENTY-SIX

THE SIGN IN ONE OF THE ROOMS OF THE Norman Rockwell museum indicated a five-person maximum capacity, and a family of five waltzed in when the limit had already been reached.

Sarah gave me her *not now* head shake, since I had a hard time curbing the desire to tell people they shouldn't stand so close or that they needed to put on a fucking mask. Neither request was all that hard. Besides, it was the principle of the thing. Give people space, and respect everyone's health. How hard was it really, fucksticks? Apparently, people didn't like me to explain they were being fucksticks.

The mother in the group pulled her mask down past her chin and let loose a loud, full-body-shaking sneeze.

"Does she not get the purpose of the mask?" I

whispered to Sarah, who was doing her best not to laugh.

"I don't think she does. Let's go to the next room." Sarah jerked her chin to the door.

"Only two are allowed, and there's a man in there."

"We only count as one."

I eyed her with suspicion. "We're two full-grown adults."

"Yes, but we're one group."

I glanced at the sign again. "Are you sure?"

"Yes. I heard the guard explain it to someone else."

"They should make the sign clearer."

"For you, yes." She took my hand.

I knew she was teasing, but I nodded because she was right. People like me needed clear directions at all times. "Does it mean five groups, then? If there are five in each group, this space will fill up well beyond what's safe."

"I think they're counting on people using common sense."

"That doesn't work." I shook my head vehemently, dropping her hand. "Not one bit."

"Common sense or yours in particular?"

I stuck my tongue out at her, but the mask hid it, resulting with me ending up with a piece of fuzz on the tip of my tongue. I persevered to say, "One of the reasons things in this country are so bad is that people aren't following simple rules."

"You stuck your tongue out at me, didn't you?"

"Yes, and I'm paying for it." I wanted to slip my fingers under the mask to pull whatever off my tongue. "I have fuzz in my mouth."

Sarah looped her arm through mine. "It does prove your common-sense theory right. A woman with a PhD and four kids still sticks her tongue out into a mask."

"It seemed wiser than screaming my head off that everyone around me is crazy."

"When you put it that way, good choice."

\* \* \*

"Why do we have to go back to the room before dinner?" I pouted. "You said we didn't have to go back until it was dark. I'm not sure I can handle seeing it in the light again."

"To change clothes," Sarah said as if that explained everything.

I glanced down at my pink shorts and *Nice Tits* T-shirt. "I'm wearing my favorite shirt, and you said it matched these shorts, which have big pockets for my phone, wallet, spare masks, and keys." I felt woozy. "Have people been making fun of me all day?"

"Honey, you match. I wouldn't let you walk out of the house looking like a fool. We have dinner plans."

"You said we're sitting outside for a picnic dinner. What gives?"

"At a fancy mansion." She waggled a finger.

"It's outside."

Sarah gave me her mom death-glare, and I wilted. "Fine, but I would like to lodge my complaint."

"Naturally. I'll file it away with all your other complaints so far this trip."

"I would stick my tongue out at you again if I didn't have to worry about fuzz." My watch beeped.

"What's that alarm for?"

"Shower."

"You showered before we left the house this morning, didn't you?"

"I know. I forgot to turn off the alarm. I wish all of you would follow the shower schedule I devised. Maddie used ours before I did. It gives me the willies." I wiggled about, feeling as if a million ants were climbing over my skin.

"I'll try to remind them." She had her back to me, but I was 99.876 percent sure she didn't mean it because she didn't follow the schedule either.

We entered the hotel room, and the shabbiness of the place gave me the heebie-jeebies all over again. "This is why I didn't want to come back to this depressing room during the day. Aside from the sneezing woman in the museum, we've been having a fantastic day."

Sarah took a bag into the bathroom. Before shutting the door, she said, "Your outfit is on top. No complaints."

"Better not be a dress!"

"Find out for yourself!" she shouted through the door.

It turned out to be a pair of capri pants and a lightweight blouse. There was a gray cardigan to go with it in case I got chilly. It didn't take long to shed my clothes and ease into the nicer outfit.

When Sarah cleared her throat to get my attention, I spun around and exclaimed, "Why didn't you tell me that was the reason for coming back to the room?"

She wore a tight black cocktail dress that emphasized all of her curves. "Because I like to see the look on your face when the penny drops."

"Can we skip the picnic?" I jerked my head to the bed.

"Nope. I also take great delight in torturing you."

I groaned, but I had to admit I liked it as well.

## CHAPTER TWENTY-SEVEN

I parked the car in the gravel lot of the mansion, and when we got out, one of the cows in the field mooed.

I flipped around, smiling, unable to pick out which beast had said hello.

"Aw, we made a friend." Sarah rested her head on my shoulder.

"The best kind."

"Dare I ask?"

"I'm pretty sure you won't let a cow move in with us." Before she could slap me or growl, I kissed her on the lips and then ordered, "Masks on!"

"You love saying that, don't you?"

"It makes me feel like I have a semblance of control over what we're calling life these days." I slipped the elastic bands over my ears.

"Shitshow. Dumpster fire. Chaos. Choose whichever one suits your mood." Sarah affixed her mask into place.

I hoisted the picnic backpack onto my shoulders, and we made our way up the elaborate cement stairs to the garden area of Naumkeag. Lights were on the railings, and off in the distance, there was guitar music.

At the check-in table, a masked woman asked for the name our reservation was under, and after Sarah supplied it, the woman ticked us off on her sheet and handed over a small bottle of red wine.

"The best table tonight is right outside the back-door of the house, and it's still available," she said in a conspiratorial voice.

I had no clue what she was talking about. Sarah and I had been there hours earlier since the house was open to visitors, but you had a limited amount of time and had to make an appointment.

Sarah made an oohing sound to the woman, and I knew it meant the tip made my wife happy. Sometimes I wondered how much I missed by focusing on the things no one else seemed to notice, like the tiny spider web under the leaves on a plant to the left of the table. Sarah was usually around for the important matters, like where we should sit to eat dinner.

We made our way to the table on the patio, and even I had to admit it was fucking impressive. The statues, water fountain, and the table, which was under grapevines on a lattice overhang.

"Look at the sunset," I said, setting the bag on a chair so I could stop and enjoy.

"These are the moments when I remember what life was like and what we have to look forward to when this pandemic ends."

I held Sarah in my arms as we turned our heads so we could press our cheeks together and watch the brilliant red-orange orb slowly descend to the horizon.

"There's something so incredibly special about a sunset, yet it happens every single day. We take it for granted almost every single day." I sighed.

"Maybe we shouldn't."

"Kinda hard with four kids, in-laws, and friends living with us. Not to mention a cat and dog."

"That's an excuse, though. We need to try harder to enjoy life."

I started to argue with Sarah, but then it dawned on me that we—or I did. Otherwise, the days would continue to slip by, turning into weeks, months, and quite possibly years without looking at another sunset. Scientists still had no idea how to tame the COVID beast, and while this weekend was turning out to be a nice getaway, I knew it would be a very long time before we could do this again. Not with winter coming, making it impossible to sit outside a mansion for a picnic.

Sarah's phone rang, and she answered the video call. "Hello, my babies." She held the phone so I could see, our faces still cheek to cheek.

"Are you guys watching the sunset?" I asked.

"No, but we can." Maddie started to shoo everyone out onto the back deck. "Oh, wow. Stunning."

"Beau-ti-ful," I recognized Freddie's voice by the awe in his tone that always alerted me to how much he understood about everything around him.

There was movement, and Rose appeared with Cal on her hip. "How's the trip?"

"It's been absolutely perfect," I said, and Sarah slipped her hand into mine. "But we miss all of you terribly and can't wait to see you tomorrow night."

After the phone was handed off to everyone to say good night, I asked, "Where's Willow?"

The screen blurred again, and I heard, "Right here."

"Thanks so much for suggesting this place. This is the most stunning picnic I've ever been on. You and Maddie should book it for next weekend. You two deserve it."

I caught a glimpse of Maddie off to the side, her smile appreciating the step I'd taken, although, I could also sense she wanted to say, "Why'd it take you so long?"

Willow nodded. "We just might do that."

The call ended, and Sarah grinned at me. "If I knew all we needed was to enjoy a sunset together for you to come around to Willow, I would have done it months ago."

"Oh, I doubt it would have worked then. I'm a bit stubborn and slow to adjust to things."

"True. When you do, though, you really do a one-eighty, taking us all by surprise and becoming the biggest cheerleader for the person you despised for so long."

"I didn't despise Willow." I unzipped the bag and fished for the green and white cloth to spread out on the table.

"You didn't like her much for a long time."

"I didn't like her being in my inner sanctum. There's a difference. I don't know how to explain it. I have a hard time pivoting to new things, people, or whatnot." I started setting the food containers on the table.

Sarah regarded me with her kind, brown eyes. "I know. I've been so worried about you."

"I'm always the problem in a group."

Sarah slanted her head. "Don't think that way. Everyone knows you're different. They love you for it. I know I do."

* * *

THE NIGHT AIR TURNED CHILLY.

"Should we head back?" I asked.

"Not yet. Do me a favor?" Sarah rifled through the other picnic bag that she hadn't let me carry or open.

"Get us a different hotel?"

"I doubt we can. Everything needs a lot more planning these days. Close your eyes."

"Why? It's pretty dark out." I glanced to my left and then right as if needing to prove it was dark.

"Lizzie!"

"Okay, okay." I closed them. "Better?"

"Don't open them until I say so."

"Fine."

The man playing guitar was off to my right, and I wondered when he would be able to call it a night.

"Open them."

I saw a cupcake with a lit candle.

"Happy birthday!"

"Aw, thanks so much."

"Go on. Make a wish."

I laughed, thinking of something, and then blew out the candle.

Sarah unwrapped her cupcake and bit into it. "Oh, this is good."

"Did you bake it?" I licked frosting off my finger.

"Yes."

"Do you think you'll continue cooking and baking after all of this is over?" I took a bite, and once I swallowed, I said, "Strawberry with cream cheese frosting. Yum."

"It's your fave. As for your question…" Sarah stared off into the darkness. "I might like to occasionally, but I am sick to death of having to cook three meals a day."

"I'm tired of running the dishwasher that many times or more each day."

"It all adds up." Sarah popped another bite of cupcake into her mouth.

The man who'd been wandering around playing guitar waved as he walked by holding his case, clearly done with his shift.

"I think they're wanting to wrap things up." I finished my birthday cupcake.

"It's past nine."

I scanned the outside of the mansion and then the patio. The only sounds were crickets and the trickling water fountain off to my right. In the distance, I saw headlights from someone heading home. "Can you imagine living here?"

"No."

We packed up our stuff and walked to the staircase while I used the flashlight app on my phone. "This was a lovely night. The whole day, actually. Thank you."

"It's not over yet."

"What else do you have planned?"

Sarah laughed. "You have to wait until we get back to the hotel."

"For—?" It hit me. "Oh, it's Sexy Sarah time."

"Are you expecting a strip show or something?"

"I wouldn't turn it down."

"You're impossible," she said, standing closer to me.

## CHAPTER TWENTY-EIGHT

By the time we got back to the hotel, I was exhausted.

I attempted to yawn without looking like I was by not moving my face too much, a trick I'd mastered as an undergrad, when I'd been forced to take classes on subject matters that went right over my head, such as astronomy, resulting with ruining my straight A average by adding a B to my GPA. It was years ago, but it still pissed me off.

Another yawn overtook me.

Sarah came out of the bathroom, still dressed and in heels. "Want to simply go to bed?"

"Uh, I remember being promised more for my birthday."

"Yes, but you look dead on your feet."

"I'm sure I can rally."

Despite her frown, she ended up laughing. "You really do have such odd seduction skills." She turned around. "Care to help me with the zipper?"

"I've been wanting to do that all night."

Sarah glanced over her shoulder. "Got a thing for zippers?"

"I like what they reveal." I started to lower hers, slowly, kissing her skin as it came to light. "Are my skills improving?"

"Keep it up, and I'll let you know."

"You say I'm impossible."

"Not all the time. Like right now."

The dress fell to the floor. "I love you in lingerie, stockings, and heels. It makes me feel terrible admitting that, considering all the advancements for women's rights, but fuck, I love this." I wrapped my arms around her, looking at our reflection in the bathroom mirror, visible through the doorway.

Sarah rested her head against me. "I think the fact that I like dressing this way frees you from guilt. You don't demand it, although you do make the occasional request."

I kissed her neck, working my way to her earlobe. "Like this?"

"It's one of your better ways of asking for things." Sarah let out a satisfied moan. "You're right. You were able to rally."

"I'm not that old yet."

"How old are you?" She flipped around, taking my breath away.

"No idea. Does it matter?"

"I find it funny that someone who loves dates can never remember her own birth year or age."

"It's all part of my charm, or possibly I can only remember so many dates." Light filtered in through the windows, and I hit the wall switch to take in the way the moonlight waltzed over her creamy skin. "You're so beautiful."

"So are you." A sexy smile overtook her lips.

Sarah captured my mouth with hers. The passion in the way she kissed me proved her previous statement.

"How'd I get so lucky?" I asked.

"I can say the same thing." She kissed me again. Hard.

My hand cupped her breast, but I needed to feel her skin, so I reached around her to unhook her bra. She helped ease the straps over her arms, and my mouth teased her nipple, making it harden.

Sarah started unbuttoning my shirt, her hand trailing down my left side. Removing it, she pulled me against her, relishing our skin touching. The heat from our bodies radiated from us.

I freed her slowly from her stockings and heels, my hands and mouth exploring her body in the process. We kissed with need, but there was tenderness as well. There always was, which filled me with the security I craved from Sarah. It was something to be told I was loved, but it meant so much more when I felt it in every cell of my body.

She undid the zipper on my capris, and they fluttered to the floor. She eased me onto the bed. Her mouth tasted my body as it explored. My hands ran up and down her back, all the while my hips started to gyrate in an insistent manner. Her tongue worked down the inside of my right leg. Back up my left.

I fucking loved it when we had the time to enjoy each other's body in all its glory, knowing no one would interrupt us. Sarah had been right. We needed this weekend away.

She moved me onto my stomach, and her fingers began to massage my lower back and then buttocks, her lips taking the occasional nip.

An excited moan escaped me. She continued massaging me, digging her fingers into my shoulders and neck. "You need this."

"You have no idea."

"I think I'm figuring it out." Her tongue flicked my earlobe, dipping into my ear.

I groaned.

"I thought you wanted a massage." She chuckled in my ear, her body pressed onto mine.

"Are you going to make me beg on my birthday?"

"As you've pointed out before, that's not actually until Tuesday."

I rolled my peepers, giving myself eyestrain. "Don't be mean!"

"Okay, okay." Sarah shifted me back over. "So demanding!"

I stared into her dark eyes. "It's part of the Sarah curse."

"Curse?" She laughed. "Please explain."

"I can never get enough of you."

"Is that right?" She continued to stare into my eyes, but a finger entered me below.

"I never want to lose you." I let out a breath, slowly.

"That's not going to happen, Lizzie. I promise." She pushed deeper, adding another finger, and eased in and out with more force.

Unable to control myself, I reached down and went inside her with a finger, causing her eyes to go wide with surprise, but she angled, making it easier for me to do. She was wet with excitement, and knowing that I was the one who turned her on this much made my eyes turn misty.

"I can't believe we're still going strong after all these years," I said through pants as we both kicked up our efforts.

"It's only going to get better." The way her body reacted to me when I was inside, always upping my eagerness. She plunged in deeper, and I matched it to the best of my ability.

We'd reached the frenzied stage of wanting to please the other, our wrists cranking to allow our fingers to move in and out. She was so wet my fingers easily slid in farther.

"Oh, Jehoshaphat!" I shouted.

Sarah's eyes widened with surprise, but she was unable to utter a word, her body quivering as much as mine. Soon enough, she came. Hard.

By the time her body stopped shaking, she fell on top of me. I wrapped my arms around her.

"Jehoshaphat?" she asked.

"It's my new thing, apparently."

"Oh, no. I know you well enough. There's a story you aren't sharing." She propped her head up on bent elbow.

I shared how Fred and I ran into the nuns.

"He's been saying fudging Christmas since that day." Sarah laughed.

The scent of sex permeated the room, allowing me the chance to inhale the enticing fragrance.

"Are you ready for sleep?" I asked in a tone that pleaded the answer would be no.

"Not yet," she whispered, stroking my cheek.

"Thank Jehoshaphat." My knee separated her legs, and I moved down to allow my mouth to take her clit.

She was already turned on, so it wouldn't take long, but I needed to taste her. From her moans, she wanted this as much as I did. She grabbed my shoulders, her fingers digging into my flesh. I reentered her, causing her to tighten her grip on me.

Sarah's moan indicated she was going to come again. She yanked my head to hers. I left my fingers inside her, and we kissed while she came.

## CHAPTER TWENTY-NINE

THE NEXT MORNING, RAIN LASHING THE window woke me from a troubled sleep.

Sarah stirred next to me.

I wrapped her into my arms and said, "Bacon."

She snuggled closer to me, laughing. "Good morning to you."

"Bacon."

"Is that really what you're thinking when naked in bed with me?" Her hand ran up my front.

"Don't try to distract me. One of your promises was I could get bacon on this trip. You've had your romantic night. Now I'm cashing in."

"*My* romantic night. It was *your* birthday."

"Technically, my birthday isn't until Tuesday." I rolled onto my side to face her.

"Can you wait five more minutes? I'm not ready to get out of bed."

"Alexa—oh, right. She's not here to set a timer, and Siri never listens to me."

"What time is it anyway?" Sarah yawned.

I looked at the nightstand, squinting since I didn't have my contacts in. "If that clock can be believed, six thirty."

"Six thirty!" she trilled. "We're on vacation!"

"I know, and you promised me bacon."

"You're as bad as the children."

"We have the greatest kids on the planet, so I'll take that as a compliment." I rolled onto my back and lifted my right arm for Sarah to settle on my chest. "Come here. I'll play your game and wait for bacon."

I could sense her eye roll, but she complied.

"It's really coming down out there." I kissed the top of Sarah's head.

"Uh-huh." From the sound of her voice, she was falling asleep, and I had two choices. Let the mother of our children enjoy sleeping in on our first weekend away and probably the only one for the year or wake her up completely for bacon.

The longer I thought about it, the bacon probably wasn't going anywhere. The hotel wasn't brimming with guests, and it was still early in the day. Odds were the bacon would last for a few more hours.

I opted to let Sarah sleep, because a grumpy Sarah for the rest of the weekend wouldn't be fun. Besides, her nakedness against me was such a delight.

I started to think about Willow. How I hadn't

been as welcoming as I could have been. The more I thought about it, the more I realized how much of a saint she'd been. Never taking my testiness to heart. Or, at least, I hoped she hadn't. All the while she was worried about losing her teaching position at the community college. After Peter told me to, I read Willow's book, and he was spot-on. It was good.

JJ had mentioned needing another historian to discuss wealth inequality since this pandemic was highlighting the disparities. A gilded age scholar was exactly what the show needed. Carefully, so as not to wake Sarah, I picked up my phone and tapped out a message to JJ, including a link to a podcast episode Willow had recently been a guest on.

It was a quarter to five in Colorado, so when I got an immediate reply saying JJ would check it out, I couldn't stop myself from asking why she was up.

*Insomnia. You?*

*Bacon.*

JJ sent a laughing emoji and then asked: *Are you going to breakfast soon?*

JJ knew I was away with Sarah for the weekend.

*No. S doesn't want to get out of bed yet.* I added a crying face.

She included a green heart emoji, which I interpreted as jealousy, followed with: *I wish I could sleep. You could go for first breakfast and then second with S without telling her. 2x the bacon.*

I mulled it over before tapping out: *That seems wrong.*

This time there were three laughing emojis and *Enjoy your weekend.*

I'd once mentioned to JJ that I didn't understand emojis, and instead of laughing at me, she'd been using them to help me figure them out since they seemed to be an important part of communication these days. And, I didn't want to accidentally make another death threat to Sarah, or anyone for that matter. Also, I think JJ found it humorous when I had to ask, *Is that one good or bad?*

I placed my phone back onto my nightstand, feeling somewhat better that I took the first step to making amends with Willow.

Now I really wanted bacon, but it'd only been minutes. Sarah would more than likely want to stay in bed for at least another hour or so, and there was no way I'd be able to turn off my brain. There was only one solution. I eased out of bed to retrieve my kindle and headphones, not wanting to waste the time.

* * *

"Bacon, Lizzie." Sarah shook me.

"What?" I rubbed my hand from the back of my head, forgetting I was wearing headphones until they crashed onto my chest with a thud.

"It's after nine. You fell asleep."

"I did?" I asked even though the evidence was literally in front of me. I hit pause on my Kindle. "Damn. I'm going to have to figure out the last thing I remember."

"Must be a riveting book." Sarah sat up, stretching her arms over her head.

"It is. Willow recommended it."

"Are you still trying to learn more than her?" Sarah slowly swiveled her head, fluttering her eyelashes and making it clear I wasn't in trouble. Not exactly, but maybe teetering on the line, although I was communicating with Willow, which was a minor victory for Sarah.

"Don't ask for miracles. I still have to be me."

Sarah shook her head, knowing it was a losing battle. "I'm starving." Her stomach rumbled.

"So, no chance for—" I looked longingly at the bed.

"Has anyone ever told you how terrible your timing is?"

"Pretty much everyone I've ever known." I ran a hand over my hair, which was getting long again since I'd been avoiding home haircuts after Troy's neo-Nazi impersonation.

"Yet you refuse to learn."

"I already told you I gotta be me. Speaking of, I have some theories about me I'd like to discuss over breakfast. But first, I need boobs."

"Bacon and now boobs?"

"It seems to be a B-word day." I placed my face into her warm cleavage.

"That doesn't bode well for your nicknames for me today." She wrapped her arms around me.

"You're the one who denied the first request of bacon, and it seems the second for a roll in the hay, so what do you expect?"

She gently shoved me to the side. "Move it, or you'll never have either again."

"You're a mean lady." I tossed the blankets off me and bounded out of bed. "Dare I use the B-word?"

"Not if you want to live. I haven't had coffee yet. I sincerely doubt I can be convicted of murder." Sarah rifled through the bag, getting clothes.

We both showered, separately to hurry up the process, and after getting dressed, we headed down the creaking carpeted stairs.

At the hostess stand, Sarah requested a table for two.

"It's still pouring," I said, turning my head to look out the windows on the front of the inn, and I was surprised I hadn't thought of this earlier when we left the room for breakfast. I chalked it up to being exhausted from the previous night, not to mention the year from hell.

"We have tables available on the patio," the woman said as if not taking my rain concern into consideration.

"Are they covered?" I asked.

Sarah tried not to smile, and the woman gave me a look that screamed, "Duh!"

"Yes, ma'am," she finally said and led us through the massive dining room. Most of the indoor tables were empty, but a few by the open windows were taken.

On the patio, which was indeed protected from the deluge, there was another couple on the far side.

Keeping my mask on, I requested a pot of tea as well as coffee for Sarah.

When the woman left, Sarah started to remove her mask, but I said, "I'd read an article that says waitstaff prefers customers to keep them on until all the ordering is done."

"That makes sense." She rehooked the straps over her ears. "Oh, they have eggs benedict." She placed the menu to the side, her selection settled.

I squirmed, not liking eggs in anything but cake or cookies. The problem was, most breakfast places had more egg options than anything else. "Pancakes and bacon for me."

"Stop the presses!" Sarah mocked.

I stuck out my tongue again, the mask shielding the action. "You know, I may start getting used to wearing these if I can keep making faces at you without you knowing."

"Aside from the fact you usually tell me, I can see in your eyes what you're doing and thinking."

"Yes, but no one else knows that I'm sticking out

my tongue. I'm an esteemed historian. My reputation needs protecting." I whacked my chest with a hand, wishing I hadn't when it smarted.

Sarah, laughing, leaned back for the coffee and tea to be situated on the table.

We placed our order, and after adding real sugar to my tea, a first since the lockdown, I finally took off my mask, my chin warm with condensation.

"Careful. People can see you now." Sarah poured milk into her coffee.

I stuck out my tongue at her.

She laughed but added, "I'll need that later, so use it sparingly."

"Are we moving onto the C-word so quickly?"

"You really do need to work on your seduction." She sipped her coffee, her eyes momentarily closing as the caffeine started its effect, but at this stage, it was mostly mental.

"But I've already bagged the hottest chick." I pointed to Sarah, who was failing miserably at her attempt to give me a snarky look. "Come on. Lighten up. We're on vacation for my birthday, meaning I get to be this way."

"Yes, I'm the uptight one."

I took a sip of my tea and shifted in my seat. "That's a good segue into what I wanted to discuss with you."

Sarah scrunched her brow but didn't speak.

"I've been doing some thinking ever since I watched a comedy special—"

"This is an odd start." She smiled in her way that conveyed *no matter what, I love you.*

"Hardy har har." I took another sip of tea, hoping the sugar would give me the courage to say what had been plaguing my mind for quite some time now. "Do you remember the Hannah Gadsby special I asked you to watch with me?"

"Yes." Sarah's face went completely blank.

"Do you remember the part where she discussed how people started telling her she may be autistic?"

She uttered another baffled yes.

"Well…" I tapped my fingernails against my teacup. "People have told me that or at least called me special or different more times than I can remember."

Sarah inhaled deeply but nodded.

"Do you think I might be… you know… on the spectrum?" I raked my hand over my head.

The stiffness around Sarah's eyes suddenly relaxed. "Would it change anything if you were?"

"Well—" I stared at the rain pounding the planter box to my left. "I don't know, but it would explain some things."

"It might, but going back to my question, what would it really change, Lizzie? You're a loving wife, a fantastic mother, and an inspirational teacher. From where I'm sitting, you have it all."

"I didn't always, though. It's been a difficult path to

this point." I tapped the side of my hand on a not-so-straight path on the white tablecloth.

Sarah reached for my hand. "I know. Let me come at it from this angle. If one of our kids was autistic, would you love them any less?"

"Not at all, but that's not where I'm coming from." I gripped my shirt over my heart. "I mean I see your point. I do. I'm just saying I struggle with forming relationships and not uttering the one thing I know I shouldn't. The wrong words continually bubble out of me at the worst moments possible."

Sarah grinned. "It's one of your most adorable traits."

"Yeah, you think so, but I don't want to hurt other people's feelings, and I have a habit of doing that."

"Okay. Tell me what you want to do. Find a specialist?"

"I don't know. I mean, like you said, I got to this point, so do I need to find out something I'd rather not know?"

"Can you put it out of your head?"

I sighed and rested my head onto my hand. "Probably not."

"That's what I thought. No matter what we decide, I want you to know I think you're wonderful the way you are."

"I think I'm starting to understand that on all levels."

Sarah cocked her head to the side. "What do you mean?"

"If I were you, I would have walked away years ago. I'm stubborn, opinionated, have a hard time admitting I'm wrong, I don't open up, I hide silly things that embarrass the hell out of me, and I tend to push a topic I know I should let go, but I can't, even when I'm chanting in my head, *Don't ask, don't ask, don't ask.*"

Sarah regarded me over her coffee cup with a quizzical expression, and I was kicking myself for supplying all the reasons she should leave.

The silence made me squirm in my seat.

After another couple of seconds, I admitted, "I would understand."

"If?" she arched one eyebrow.

"If you left."

Her expression didn't change, and she took another sip of coffee. "Do you really think you listed things I didn't already know?"

"Probably not. But it's out there now. There's a possibility, a very strong one, I'm on the spectrum. You can't pull back from that once you've opened the door."

"Don't even think of pulling back from me or anything. That goes against your personality. You love to put your head down and keep going, no matter what." She acted this out, making me smile.

"I should keep listening to the audiobooks I got on the subject, then?"

Sarah burst into laughter, but she quickly covered her mouth. She muttered, "I should have known," between the cracks of her fingers.

"What?"

"That's always your first step. Buy books and research the hell out of it. Thank God you didn't major in psychology. You would have spent all those years thinking you had every mental disease in the textbooks."

"I've never considered myself a Nazi, so there might be a flaw in your thinking. I've been studying them all of my adult life."

The waitress buzzed by with a refill for Sarah's coffee, and I thought I detected her flinching when she overheard the word Nazi, but not the other pertinent words that I wasn't one.

Sarah sucked her lips into her mouth, trying not to laugh her head off.

After the woman retreated inside, I said, "I know. Don't mention Nazis in public unless in a classroom."

"It's the safest bet these days, considering."

I fiddled with an unopened sugar pack. "So, what's your verdict?"

"I don't think you're a Nazi." Sarah rested on her forearms.

I snorted. "You know that wasn't what I was asking."

She reached for my hand. "Lizzie, I love you. No matter what. Forever."

CHAPTER THIRTY

We stood in the impressive French Flower Garden of The Mount, Edith Wharton's home, the water from a fountain trickling and a slight breeze cooling us off.

"It's amazing isn't it?" I said, my eyes taking in the different flowers, ranging from lilies to hydrangea and sculpted shrubs, providing bursts of colors against a deep azure sky.

Sarah nodded.

"I mean. It's so beautiful and alive, which only highlights how dark this year has been so far. We spend the majority of our time indoors."

Sarah's phone trilled, shattering the peacefulness. She reached into her bag, answering it as I waved an apologetic hand to the other couple on the far side of the garden.

She moved off to the side, speaking to Maddie since I heard Sarah say the name.

I continued gazing at all the colors, wondering what it must have been like to live here all those years ago.

"She did what?" Sarah flipped around, and my body tensed.

I didn't know what they were talking about, but from Sarah's narrowing gaze, I knew I was the subject.

I scanned my memory bank to seize upon the moment where I'd gone wrong, but nothing came to mind aside from our spectrum conversation at breakfast. There was no way Maddie knew about that, so I continued to gawk in a *what I'd do now* way.

Gauging from Sarah's body language, I wasn't actually in trouble. Quite the opposite, since her eyes were filling with happy tears. In the beginning of our relationship, I probably wouldn't have guessed those were the result of joy, but after all this time, I'd stake my life on the fact.

"We'll be home tonight." Sarah finished with the call.

I waited to see what the whole hullabaloo was about.

Sarah slipped her phone back into her bag. "I can't believe you."

"Why?" I reached for her hand, and we started walking back along the gravel walkway with linden trees flanking both sides.

"You got Willow a job."

I stopped in my tracks. "I what?"

"You didn't know JJ called Maddie to speak with Willow?"

"Nope."

"But JJ said you gave her the idea."

"When JJ and I were texting earlier today while you slept, I mentioned Willow and how she'd be a good fit considering her specialty." I paused as the words started to click together. "Wait. JJ hired Willow today?"

Sarah nodded, threading her arm through mine. "You're amazing."

"Why didn't Maddie call me?"

"She tried. Your phone must be off."

"I forgot to pack the charger," I confessed.

"You can use the one in the car on the way home." Sarah stopped, her eyes sweeping the garden one last time. "This has been a wonderful weekend."

"It has. Thank you."

She turned her head to mine. "Happy birthday."

We kissed briefly, but since we wore masks, it was more a peck than anything.

"It's a shame we have to leave such a beautiful place," I said.

"Yes."

Sarah started to turn around, but I tugged on her arm.

"Uh… can we not mention the possible autism thing to anyone until…?" I boosted a shoulder.

"I won't say a thing." She placed a finger to her mask.

"I'm scared."

"I know, honey."

"Not just because of that, but we still don't know when this pandemic will end."

"It's going to be months before we make progress on that front, I think." Sarah's voice was filled with emotion, anger being the overwhelming one. "But we can only control how we react. I know we'll weather this like we do everything else."

"Bumpy?" I asked.

She quietly laughed before saying, "Together."

"I like the sound of that."

She took my hand. "You ready?"

I looked up at the house, then the sky, and, finally, the dirt road leading to the parking lot. "Let's go home."

A HUGE THANK YOU!

First, thanks so much for reading *A Woman Trapped*. I feel like I should state right now for those who love Lizzie and her adventures in life, yes, there will be another story in the series. It'd be cruel to stop now, right when Lizzie is learning crucial details about herself and why she does some of the things she does.

When I published the first book in the A Woman Lost series, I had no idea the impact Lizzie would have on so many. I've received countless emails from readers who have confessed how much Lizzie means to them. It wasn't until I announced the end of the series that I realized how many love her. I have to admit while it's flattering, it's also intimidating, because I fear I'll eventually mess up the Lizzie arc, letting down readers.

However, that's the risk a writer has to take with

every single story they publish. I've published more than twenty novels, and I still find it simply amazing that people read my stories. When I hit publish on my first book back in 2013, after staring at the publish button for several days before I worked up the nerve to finally press it, I had no idea what would happen.

Seven years later, I still panic when I'm about to publish a new project, but it's because of your support that I find the courage to do it. My publishing career has been a wonderful journey, and I wouldn't be where I am today without you cheering me on.

If you enjoyed the story, I would really appreciate a review. Even short reviews help immensely.

Finally, don't forget if you want to stay in touch, sign up for my newsletter. I'll send you a free copy of *A Woman Lost* (just in case you don't have it yet), book 1 in the A Woman Lost series, plus the bonus chapters and *Tropical Heat* (a short story), all of which are exclusive to subscribers. And, you'll be able to enter monthly giveaways to win one of my books.

You'll also be one of the firsts to hear about many of my misadventures, like the time I accidentally ordered thirty pounds of oranges, instead of five. To be honest, that stuff happens to me a lot, which explains why I own three of the exact same *Nice Tits* T-shirt, just like Lizzie. In case you're wondering, the shirt has pictures of the different tits of the bird variety because I have some pride.

Here's the link to join: http://eepurl.com/hhBhXX

And, thanks again for letting Lizzie into your hearts.

## ABOUT THE AUTHOR

TB Markinson is an American who's recently returned to the US after a seven-year stint in the UK and Ireland. When she isn't writing, she's traveling the world, watching sports on the telly, visiting pubs in New England, or reading. Not necessarily in that order.

Her novels have hit Amazon bestseller lists for lesbian fiction and lesbian romance. For a full listing of TB's novels, please visit her Amazon page.

Feel free to visit TB's website to say hello (lesbianromancesbytbm.com). On the *Lesbians Who Write* weekly podcast, she and Clare Lydon dish about the good, the bad, and the ugly of writing. TB also runs I Heart Lesfic, a place for authors and fans of lesfic to come together to celebrate and chat about lesbian fiction.

Want to learn more about TB. Hop over to her *About* page on her website for the juicy bits. Okay, it won't be all that titillating, but you'll find out more.

Printed in Great Britain
by Amazon